SHEER

A HOLLYWOOD ROMANCE

SARAH ROBINSON

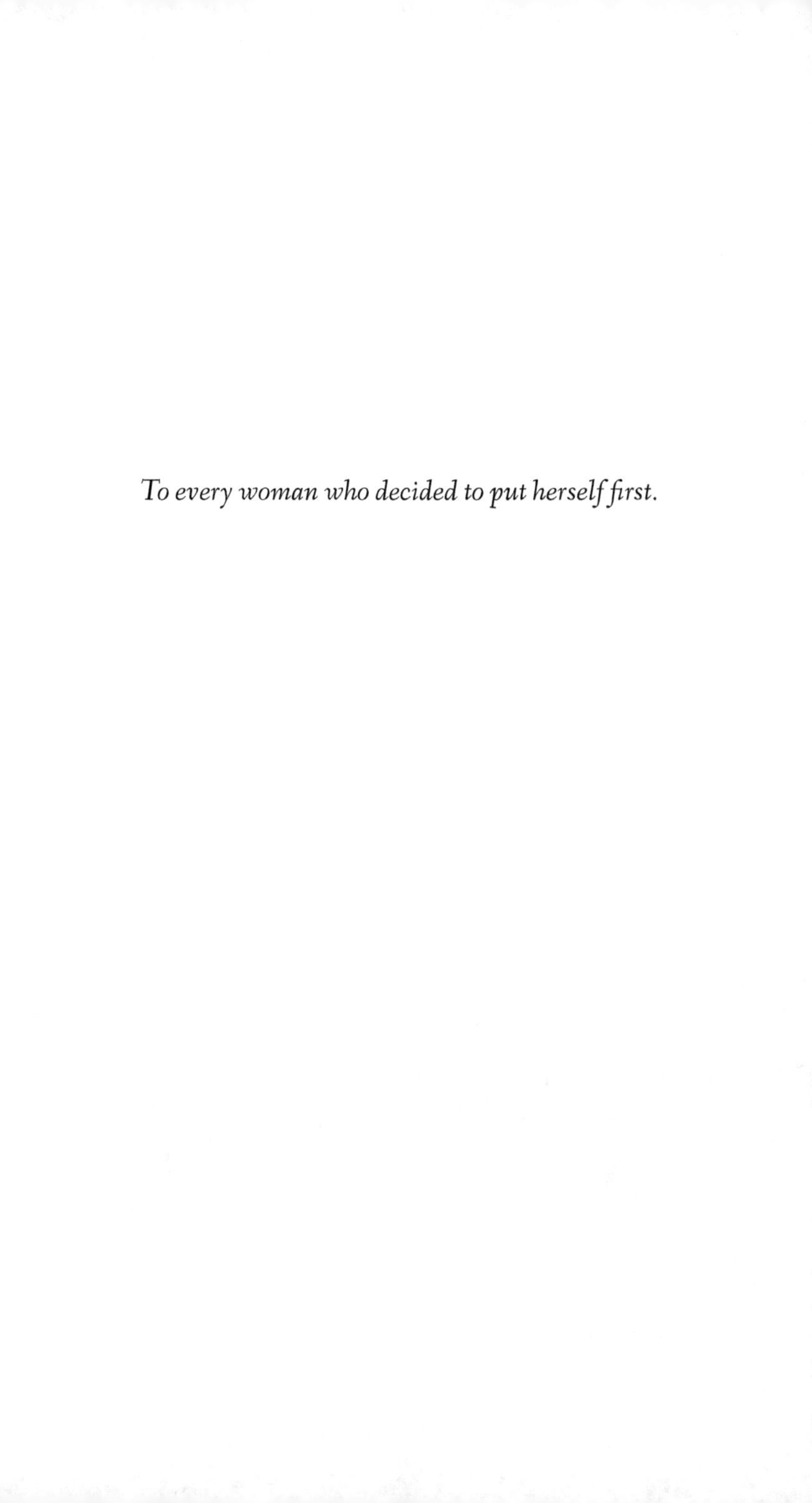

To every woman who decided to put herself first.

CHAPTER ONE

"THAT'S a big package you've got there," the young woman seated at the desk outside a large wooden door said. A teasing smile played on her lips.

Grant Mercer glanced down at the cardboard box in his hands. "I'm here to see Mr. Lawson," he said, ignoring her earlier statement.

She bristled at his rough tone, and for a moment, he felt he should apologize for almost barking at her, but then he decided against it. Frankly, he just didn't care what she or anyone else thought of him.

"Your name?" she asked, still looking up at him demurely. "Sir?"

He was more than used to receiving attention from women wherever he went, but it still never felt natural. With his physical attributes—thick blond, wavy hair pulled into a loose bun at the back of his head and deep green eyes that always gave away what he was feeling—he'd never had a shortage of women if he'd wanted them. Being a playboy, however, had never been his thing. While he'd had plenty of experience in his past, he tended to be more introverted and kept to himself when he could.

"Grant Mercer."

Her face lit up. "Oh, he's expecting you, Mr. Mercer. Go on in."

"Thanks." Grant readjusted the large box in his arms then gripped the door knob and stepped inside the luxurious movie producer's office.

A man with short brown hair and a hint of stubble across his chin was seated at a large glass desk in front of an entire wall of windows overlooking Los Angeles behind him. The man lifted his chin and smiled at him. "Grant Mercer?"

Grant nodded and placed his box on a nearby chair. "That's me."

"Ben Lawson," the man said as he stood and walked around the desk. He offered his hand to Grant as he came closer. "How was your flight from New Zealand?"

"It was actually quite pleasant, surprisingly." Though that really had more to do with what he was leaving behind in New Zealand than it did with arriving in America.

"Good." Ben motioned toward a plush chair across the desk from his. "Make yourself comfortable. Would you like a scotch? Whiskey?"

Grant shrugged. "Whatever you're having." While he knew he wasn't the friendliest guy out there, he was definitely going to be on his best behavior for his boss. The guy was paying him high six figures for barely a month's work, so if that meant he had to turn his usual frown into a smile, he'd fucking do it. He needed this job a lot more than he'd like to admit.

Ben picked up a glass bottle from a bar cart set to one side of the room. "Scotch it is."

A minute later, he'd returned to the desk and offered the glass to Grant. Grant took a sip, then set it down on the desk top as Ben returned to his seat across from him.

"So, *Kiss Me, Kate.*" Ben opened a drawer and pulled out a large stack of papers, handing it to him. "Here's a copy of the latest manuscript."

The project title was written across the front, and Grant flipped through a few pages, scanning the dialogue. "It's such a classic. Doing a modern-day version of this musical is going to be stunning."

Ben nodded his head. "I agree. It's been a bit of a passion project of mine, honestly. However, the key to making this movie a hit is going to be the score. Especially considering that we're doing the entire thing live."

"That's where I come in," Grant replied, smiling for the first time since stepping foot in America. Music was where he shone, and as one of the most sought-after film composers in the business, he had no doubt that he was going to make this movie shine. "The melodies and lyrics are already set from the classical version and the Broadway show, but we're going to set it to modern day beats and instruments. It'll be like entirely new songs."

"That's what I'm counting on." Ben turned his computer screen around so Grant could see it. "I'll show you some footage from our casting sessions. The leads are already in place, and we're just working on flushing out the rest of the characters. We'll be ready to start official rehearsals within the month."

"So, you'll need all the music ready by then?"

"Do you think you can make that work?" Ben asked. "The background score is secondary, so we can wait until pre-production on that, but the songs need to be ready for the actors. Though, they're already ready with the lyrics as they've been told to practice the classic versions."

"It's not a problem," Grant assured him, then gestured toward the cardboard box he'd been carrying. "I actually have more than half of it ready to go. The sheet music is all there. I'd definitely love to get started with the leads as soon as possible to work out the kinks."

"Perfect." Ben pointed at the computer screen and clicked play on the video he'd pulled up. "This is our lead actress, Simone Reynolds."

One of the classical songs from the original version came through the speakers, a soft and stunning piece made only more beautiful by the woman singing it. "Her voice is stunning," Grant said, feeling drawn to her voice. It was a testament to the singer they'd cast, because her talent was unparalleled.

"Isn't it?" Ben skipped forward to another part of the video, eager to hear more of her range in another song. "She just came off of winning third place in the *American Voice* singing competition literally two weeks ago, but despite not coming in first, she was the clear audience favorite."

Grant had to admit that he'd watched a few episodes of her season streaming online, and she'd certainly been his favorite pick as well. Not only was she gorgeous and an incredible singer, but her spunky personality came through in every scene, and it was exactly the kind of endearing persona that audiences ate up. "That's great PR for this film."

Ben nodded. "We're already hearing buzz for this film, so we're hoping it hits ratings hard. Full disclosure, however, Simone is my wife's younger sister."

Grant chuckled, but he didn't blame the executive for the potential nepotism. Simone was clearly perfectly suited for the role and had the vocals to match. He could definitely work with her range and was already excited to see how far he could push her. "There's no judgment here from me. The woman can sing."

"Exactly," Ben replied. "Come on. We'll head down to the studio, and you can meet. She should be working with her voice coach around now."

Grant stood and moved to pick up his box of sheet music.

"Leave that here. I'll have my secretary bring it to your office. You're going to love your set up—full office, studio, soundproof booth, every instrument in existence, the whole nine yards."

"I can't wait to see it," Grant replied. While he did have an amazing setup at his luxurious cliffside home in New Zealand where he composed most of his work, there was something to be said for using the top-of-the-line equipment that large production companies like this one could offer him. Not to mention the fact that he couldn't stay in New Zealand to work on this project even if he wanted to.

He tried to push the thoughts of those demons away. He didn't have time to think about what was waiting for him back home.

"I'll take you there after you meet Simone," Ben confirmed, ushering him out of the office. "Lydia, can you take Mr. Mercer's things to his office?"

The young receptionist jumped to her feet and smiled at Grant. "Of course, Mr. Lawson. Anything Mr. Mercer needs."

Ben chuckled as they got onto the elevator. "I think you're going to have a lot of fun in Hollywood, Grant."

He grinned but shook his head. "Nah. That's not my style."

"Good," Ben replied. "I like a man who keeps work at the forefront. No distractions."

Ironically, looking for a distraction was the entire reason he'd taken this job in the first place. "Exactly."

"That's how I met my wife, though. My first project here at Shepherd Films, and she was definitely a distraction," he joked, though the sappy in-love expression on his face was enough to make Grant want to gag. "You've got someone back home waiting for you?" Ben asked.

Grant shook his head. "Just a bonsai tree that I left with a neighbor to take care of and an ex-wife who ran off with my best friend and everything I own."

He realized how pathetic that sounded even as it came out of his mouth but it was too late to take it back.

Ben cleared his throat. "That sounds...I'm sorry...well, um...bonsais are nice."

Great. Now his new boss thought he was an idiot. He didn't even know why he'd admitted to all of that, but fucking hell, it was out there now. "I mean, well, yeah. Bonsais are nice."

They rode the rest of the elevator ride in silence, finally coming to the lobby and going out to the security desk. They climbed onto a golf cart and Ben steered them across the lot to a large warehouse-type building with a sign reading "Studio D" across the top. The entire campus was shockingly large, and despite the fact that he'd worked on dozens of movies in Hollywood, he always got lost getting around the vast lots and studios.

Entering the warehouse, Grant noted immediately that it was full of bustling personnel shouting across the open space as they hammered and built. His eyes widened at the utter chaos of it all, and yet, somehow everyone knew what they were doing and where they were going.

"They're currently building the sets for the movie," Ben explained loudly over the volume of the studio. He pointed toward a few different areas, explaining what each of those locations was going to be by the time filming started. "Ah, there's Simone."

Grant followed Ben's gesture to a woman dangling from a long piece of white silk suspended from the high beams above. Short dark hair with red streaks stood out against the white silk, and tattoos spread across her back and one arm. Her knee was bent around the fabric while the rest of her hung below, twisting in the air.

As they got closer, Grant heard the man standing a few feet underneath her instructing her to project louder.

"How loud can I possibly be upside down?" she snapped back. "I'm singing to the floor."

Grant tried not to laugh at her snarky response. He struggled not to notice how gorgeous she looked in a tight leotard and leggings that perfectly contoured her figure. Long, muscular legs stretched out over her upside-down small waist and perfect round breasts, she was as hypnotic to look at as she was to hear sing.

"From the top," the man continued, ignoring her complaints.

She sighed and swung her second leg up over the fabric just as Ben called out to her. "Simone!"

Her leg faltered as her gaze was pulled toward Ben, and she suddenly slipped from the fabric's embrace. The man beneath her stepped backwards, as if to avoid her falling on him.

Jumping forward, Grant reached out and caught her in his arms as she tumbled, just before she hit the ground.

"Ah!" She gasped, the wind clearly knocked out of her at the impact against his arms. She coughed and held her chest as he lowered her feet to the ground. Wide, bright brown eyes stared back at him as she caught her breath and a soft pink painted over her cheeks.

"Are you okay?" Grant asked her, ignoring the fact that the man who had been coaching her was now rushing over like he'd given a crap in the first place.

"Simone, are you okay?" the man asked.

"Step back," Grant said to him, his hand still on Simone's waist as she steadied herself. Grant wanted to punch the idiot in the face. "You were going to let her fucking fall."

The man put his hands up but didn't move away. "It happened so fast! That's not my fault."

Grant shot the coward a piercing glare. "I said *step back.*"

"Okaaaay... Everyone calm down." Ben intervened, putting a hand on Simone's shoulder. Grant let go and gave him room. Ben turned to Simone. "Simmy, how are you feeling?"

She nodded her head slowly. "Fine. Just caught me by surprise is all."

Ben frowned, still looking worried. He waved over a production assistant wearing a headset walking by. "Hey, put in an order for a mat for when Ms. Reynolds is doing her aerial silk."

"Ben, the entire purpose is to not need safety measures," Simone tried to interject. "It's all about talent and precision."

"When you get some talent, then maybe you don't need a mat," Grant replied for Ben.

Ben laughed, but Simone looked ready to murder him as she cut her eyes his direction. "I'll have you know that I've been practicing for years," she informed him. "And I'm very good at it."

Grant crossed his arms over his chest and leveled his gaze at her. He wasn't about to miss out on a pay day he desperately needed because the lead actress had a death wish. "Sure, if you don't count almost falling to your death."

"Simone, this is Grant Mercer. He's the composer for *Kiss Me, Kate*, and you'll be working with him on your musical numbers." Ben pointed between the two. "And Grant, this is Simone Reynolds, our lead."

She put out her hand toward him, her red-streaked hair falling forward across her shoulder as she reached out. "It's nice to meet you."

From her tone, he didn't believe for a second that she thought meeting him was nice at all. Clearly, she'd forgotten the whole saved-her-life-a-few-seconds-ago thing. "Charmed," he replied, shaking her hand. "And you're welcome."

Her nostrils flared, but she gave a small nod, her chin pointed high. "Thanks for catching me."

He grinned, seeing how hard that admission must have been for her. As annoying as she'd already proven to be, he had to admit that he was starting to look forward to working with her. She was every bit the wild spirit he'd seen on television, and there was nothing more fun than challenging a woman who would certainly never back down from a fight.

CHAPTER TWO

"HE IS LITERALLY INFURIATING," Simone said to her older sister, Teagan, as they stood on the local playground watching her two nieces running around the different structures, playing tag. "I cannot believe Ben invited him to dinner."

Teagan shrugged. "He's just being nice. The poor guy doesn't know anyone here, and Aria told me he's going through a divorce."

Simone raised her brows. "Really?"

"Yep," Teagan replied, then waved her hand toward her daughter, Piper, and Aria's daughter, Tillie, where they had moved to playing in the sandbox. "Piper! Don't throw sand at your cousin!"

"You made me eat sand once," Simone reminded her, chuckling.

Teagan laughed. "Let's hope the sins of the mother are not genetic," she replied. "Piper's been struggling to adjust to Reed being gone. She's always asking for Daddy, and it breaks my heart."

Simone put an arm around her sister's shoulder. "When does he get back from filming?"

"A month," Teagan said with a sigh. "But we're going to visit him in Paris next weekend."

"The life of actors," she replied. "I don't know how you all do it."

"Hey, you're an actress now, too." Teagan propped her hand on her hip. "You're going to be jet setting around the world soon enough."

"I'm a singer who just happens to be acting in this particular project," Simone pointed out. "After this, maybe I'll move to New York with you guys and sing on Broadway."

"Two Reynolds sisters on Broadway?" Teagan laughed. "Get ready, world!"

"We could start our own show with all three of us sisters. Make a whole production of it all." Simone fluffed her fingers through her hair, letting the wavy curls fall around her face. "We could make bank."

Teagan shook her head. "Aria would never move to New York, especially now that Mom needs us here."

Sadness draped over the moment as Simone thought about how their family had fallen apart so recently. As much as she loved having Teagan and Piper here in Los Angeles for a while, she hated the reason they'd come.

"Is there anything else we need to plan for the memorial?" Simone asked, leaning down to pick a dandelion from the grass. She blew on it, watching the tiny buds float away with the wind. For a sliver of a second, she wished she could float away like that, carefree and off to build a new life in new grass. None of the pain and responsibility of her life now pulling at her.

Teagan shook her head. "No. Dad already had everything planned before he died. Everything is exactly the way he wanted it."

"He always was a planner," Simone replied.

After over a decade of being wheelchair bound from multiple sclerosis, their father had died two weeks ago from complications. It was sudden and not...expected and shocking. There was something about that dichotomy that seemed right for their family.

There'd been a small funeral two days after his passing for the immediate family, but his memorial would be on the one month anniversary of his passing and open to all. It was expected to draw a large crowd. Despite his lack of mobility, their father had headed up multiple charity boards and nonprofits, constantly working to leave the world a better place once he left. And that was exactly what he had done.

"Hey, Simmy?" Teagan pulled her down onto a bench as they continued to keep a mindful eye on the little girls. "Can I tell you a secret?"

"Obviously. I'm a vault." That was actually true. As the baby of the family, she was often overlooked while her more outgoing older sisters took the spotlight. While she hated that lack of attention, it did afford her the privilege of hearing a lot of secrets and always being in the background. She never shared, of course, but she loved knowing that people came to her when they needed their stories held close.

Teagan glanced sideways at her, visibly swallowing hard. "I...I'm pregnant."

"Teag!" Simone threw her arms around her sister, wrapping her in a hug. "That's amazing!"

"I know," Teagan replied, but she was sniffling and tears were beginning to line her lower lashes. "But...but I knew a month ago. I knew, and it was still early, so we waited."

Simone leaned back, that familiar heaviness settling on her chest. "You wished you'd told Dad."

The two women were quiet for a moment, looking forward and watching Piper dump sand on Tillie's sandcastle. Only a few weeks ago, those two little girls had been on their grandfather's lap as he read them bedtime stories. They'd been laughing and smiling, not a care in the world because no one knew what was about to happen.

Simone's heart squeezed as she thought of her father never knowing about his future granddaughter or grandson. Or how he'd never meet the children she'd one day have, or the man she'd one day marry. How he'd miss out on weddings and birthdays and graduations and everything that brought family together.

"I wasn't ready, Simmy," Teagan whispered, squeezing her hand. "I thought we had more time."

She nodded, trying hard to swallow the lump forming in her throat and push back the tears that wanted to spill. This wasn't who she was. She wasn't a crier, and she certainly wasn't the type to spill emotion everywhere. And yet, the last two weeks had been nothing but that.

Her father had been everything to her. Being the last daughter to move out of the house had given her a special relationship with their parents. She'd gotten more attention, more time, more one-on-one from both her mother and father, and it was a time she cherished. But it also meant that now that he was gone, one of the pillars in her life had suddenly vanished. One of the people who'd formed who she was...gone.

A flash suddenly caught the corner of her eye and Simone turned to find the source. A man with a camera was sticking out from behind a bush at the edge of the playground. "Fuck. Teag, look."

Her sister quickly spotted the man. "Paparazzi. I swear to God, sometimes I hate being famous."

"They could be here for me, you know," Simone teased, though she knew it was a lot more likely they were following her sister around after Teagan had starred in a series of dance films that had quickly become a cult classic and brought her and Reed together in front of adoring fans' eyes.

Teagan laughed. "Let's get the girls and head home."

Simone glanced down at her watch. "Do you think Mom's up yet?"

"I doubt it," Teagan replied. "She's barely left her bed. Hell, I know I wouldn't if Reed died. You'd have to peel me off his grave."

"Yeah..." Simone agreed, though admittedly, she didn't know what that felt like. She'd watched her sisters fall in love, and she loved her brothers-in-laws, but she didn't even remotely understand what it was like to be so wrapped up in another person. "I don't know what that's like."

"What about Peter?" Teagan asked. "You were head over heels for him."

"That wasn't real love. That was a hit-and-run heartbreak." Simone shuddered at the memory of the first man she'd thought she truly loved. Instead, he'd used her to get close to her agent on his mission to become famous. Her agent had told him he couldn't sign him since it was a conflict of interest to work with them both. Peter decided the solution was to break up with her.

Thankfully, her agent still refused to sign him.

The entire experience had left a bad taste in her mouth. Trust seemed out of the question now—everyone she even considered dating seemed to have ulterior motives. She realized that she didn't truly understand what *in love* felt like, and she'd certainly never felt anything close with Peter or anyone else.

No one had ever made her feel that spark, that intensity that she'd seen in her sisters' relationships or even in her parents'. No one ever made her feel like it was worth it to step out on the ledge and risk everything for someone who might be...nothing.

That fire was what she wanted more than anything.

A pair of deep green eyes suddenly crossed her mind, and she felt a small flicker of nerves in her stomach as her thoughts drifted to the man who'd caught her mid-fall yesterday. Despite how infuriating he'd been, she had to admit that she'd been a little taken with his saving-the-damsel-in-distress act, which really pissed her off because she was very I-am-woman-hear-me-roar. But he hadn't even hesitated to put himself into harm's way to catch a complete stranger...and then she'd gotten a look at him.

If the air hadn't already been knocked out of her, his face would have made her just as breathless. A strong, thick jaw with a hint of stubble and dark green irises that looked like they'd seen more than their fair share of heartbreak...he was somehow as transparent as he was mysterious. She couldn't pinpoint anything about him, and yet his face was so expressive, so giving that she felt like everyone knew him from just a look.

She couldn't even think about his accent, which she'd later found out was from New Zealand. The way he spoke made her skin tingle and her heart beat speed up, and she wasn't really sure she could handle an entire dinner listening to him.

"Piper! Don't pull Tillie's hair!" Teagan swung her daughter up into her arms, propping her on her hip. "Simmy, can you get Tillie?"

Simone quickly pushed away her thoughts of Grant, chiding herself on letting herself get carried away like that, even if for only a moment. She lifted Aria's daughter into her arms, and the sisters headed back toward the parking lot to find Teagan's car.

"So, what's the dress code for dinner tonight?" Simone asked as they walked, trying to not sound very obvious.

Teagan gave her a funny look. "Same things we wear every week for the last twenty years?"

"I know." Simone shrugged as they reached the car. Teagan began buckling Piper into her car seat while Simone moved around to the other side and did the same with Tillie. "But, we don't normally have guests."

Okay, that wasn't entirely true. Her family loved to invite every newcomer to Los Angeles over for dinner. In fact, most family dinners had at least one or two non-related guests every week.

"Yeah, we do." Teagan finished with Piper and climbed into the driver's seat. Suddenly she paused and turned to look at Simone as she sat in the passenger side. "Oooh. Simmy!"

"What?" She could already feel her face turning bright red.

Teagan pulled the car into reverse and backed out of the space. "Are you crushing on this Grant guy?"

"No!" Simone quickly looked away, opting to watch the scenery out the window as they headed back home. "I was just asking what I should wear."

"Simmy, I love you, but you've never asked me what to wear before in your life. Your hair is a different color every few weeks, half of you is tattoos, and your wardrobe looks like a vintage clothing shop threw up on you."

"Tell me how you really feel," Simone replied sarcastically. "But I do not like Grant. He was a complete jerk yesterday. He told me I had no talent on the silk."

Her sister paused a moment. "Well, that is kind of rude. You've been practicing that for years."

"Thank you!" Simone put out her hands like that's exactly what she'd been saying all along. "I'm not a pro, but I'm still damn good."

"All right, then screw this guy." Teagan gave her a smile that said she still didn't believe her. "And then just wear whatever you want. Who cares what he thinks?"

Simone nodded. "Of course. Right. I will."

Except she hated that somewhere in the back corners of her mind, she did kind of care a little what the tall, handsome stranger with the gorgeous accent thought.

CHAPTER THREE

"I'M TRYING to keep you out of jail, Grant," his lawyer, Andrew Wilson, said through the phone. "You've got to work with me here. The divorce is finalized, but your legal troubles are far from over."

"I'm not going to fucking jail," Grant seethed into the phone, though he knew that it was a very real possibility at this point. "Listen, you're my lawyer. I'm paying you a shit ton of money to fix this. So, fix it."

With that, he hung up the phone and shoved it back into his pocket. He didn't have time to deal with the giant mess he'd left behind in New Zealand right now. He had a job to do and a payday to collect. That's all this trip to Los Angeles was for him, honestly.

He sat back down at the keyboard and glanced up at the clock. He still had a little time before Ben would be here and they'd be heading back to his house for dinner. Grant still couldn't believe he'd even agreed to go, but when the boss asked...

That was a lie. It really had nothing to do with Ben asking at all.

If he was being honest, he wanted to see Simone again, and even more than that, he wanted to see where she came from. He wanted to see what she was really like in her home and around her family, because the woman he'd met had a million walls up around her. But on her turf? He was sure he'd see the real Simone there, and not only was that going to be good for their work together, but he was personally intrigued by the acrobatic singer.

Strange, since honestly, he was nowhere near ready to move on from the bitterness and resentment he'd been filled with since his divorce. Sure, he was over his marriage. He didn't love his ex-wife, Serena, anymore, and that part of his life was long behind him. But the betrayal of his best friend *and* the woman he'd loved? Not to mention the legal disaster they'd left in their wake?

He wasn't fucking over that. In fact, he was a little angry at the entire world for that.

His fingers danced over the keyboard piano keys angrily as he paused every few moments to write down a new note or chord on the sheet music beside him. He could get lost like this for hours. He could soothe those jagged edges in the melodies he composed, but the moment the song ended, so did his peace.

Another hour passed before Grant finally looked up from his work. Just as he did, there was a knock on the studio door behind him.

"Grant?"

He turned to see Simone standing in the doorway, her knuckles wrapping around the open door. She was wearing a short dress, black with pink polka dots, and she had a single pink streak in her short hair to match. The way her curls bobbed around her chin, her shoulders bare and showing off the dark lines of ink that circled half of her body, made him pause for a moment to take in how different she looked now compared to when she'd been wearing her spandex-tight outfit from a few days ago. Everything about the way she looked, the way she dressed, screamed her personality, and he loved how she put every part of who she was on display like that.

Finally, he cleared his throat and greeted her. "Hi."

A soft blush crept up her cheeks, though he could tell she was trying hard to hide it. "Ben asked me to give you a ride to dinner. He got caught up in a work emergency."

Grant nodded, putting down his pencil and standing. "Sure. I appreciate the ride."

"No point paying for a Lyft when we're all going to the same place," she mused, stepping out of his way so he could move into the hall beside her.

"Or Uber," he added. "We don't have Lyft where I live in New Zealand yet."

"Seriously? That's a shame."

He shrugged, not really caring one way or the other. "It's not that big a deal."

"For moral reasons, I only take Lyft. But also, I like my life and plan on staying alive. Lyft actually has driver standards." Simone walked outside with him and pointed toward her car. "I'm over there."

"You are very opinionated, you know that?" he told her as they walked the rest of the distance to her car and climbed inside.

She buckled herself into the driver's seat. "Is there something wrong with that?"

He shook his head. "No. I kind of like it, actually. You're not boring and vacant like a lot of Hollywood actresses can be. This town hasn't gotten to your head."

"What do you know about Hollywood? Some say this is

where all the greatest social revolutions have started," she argued, pointing the car toward the freeway. "Hollywood may be glitz and glamor, but it has its substance."

"Sweetheart, I may be from another country, but I've been around this block enough times to know that it's a lot of silicone and hairspray."

Simone glanced sideways at him briefly, her eyes narrowed. "You are very opinionated, you know that?"

He laughed at the fact that she'd thrown his line back in his face. "Is there something wrong with that?"

"Yes. It's annoying," she replied. "Everything out of your mouth is negative."

He couldn't argue with her on that one. Hell, his entire life right now was negative, so of course his attitude was going to lean that direction. "Not a lot to be positive about these days."

She seemed to soften a bit at his admission. "I...I heard about your divorce. I'm really sorry."

He shrugged off her words. "It's fine. It's over."

"Do you *feel* over it?" she asked. "Was it recent?"

This time he was the one who was annoyed. "It's really none of your business, don't you think?"

"Fine." She turned her attention back to the road. "Be all elusive and miserable. See if I care."

They sat in silence for another ten minutes or so and he watched California pass by his window, trying to puzzle together why he'd been so short with her. She was clearly just trying to be nice, but he really hadn't spoken to anyone about his divorce. Hell, he'd barely even explained it to his own parents. He'd just stated that they were over, and not shared any more details.

He certainly hadn't told anyone how she'd broken his heart, stolen his best friend, and left him on the brink of being arrested the moment he landed back in New Zealand.

Grant turned to look at Simone. Her face was hard, her knuckles clenched tightly around the steering wheel.

"I *am* over it," he finally admitted to her.

She didn't respond or move a muscle.

"I am over *her*," he amended. "The marriage is done and I'm glad, but there's more to the situation than just broken vows, and I don't know if I'll ever get over that."

Her tongue slid across her lower lip. "Well, even though it's none of my business, I'm sorry you're going through it."

"Thanks."

"How long do you plan to stick around here?" she asked, turning down a long driveway at the top of a hill.

"I'll be here for a while. Maybe a month." He sighed. "Believe me, I'm not eager to go home anytime soon."

"I've never really understood that feeling," she told him, her hand smoothing over her dress, adjusting it to cover her knees as she drove. "I've always lived in Los Angeles, and never really ventured...anywhere. I haven't even traveled much."

That surprised him given how prominent her family was and the wealth she had at her fingertips. "Do you want to travel?"

She nodded quickly. "Definitely. I'd *love* it, but it just never seems to work out—timing-wise."

"You're so young—what, twenty-five?" he asked.

She nodded. "Twenty-six."

"So there's more than enough time to travel. Especially now when you have no commitments."

Simone laughed, her chin tilting upward as the sound bellowed dryly from her chest. It was hollow and empty, and something about the sound made him sad for her. "No commitments. I wish."

"I mean kids and a husband and all that. Those things will tie you down—believe me." He didn't have any kids of his own, but God knew they'd tried. The reminder sent a twinge of pain through his heart at the pregnancy they'd lost only two years ago—how different things had been then.

"There are more types of commitments than just those," she replied, her gaze trained straight ahead at the road. "First, my sister was injured and everything revolved around taking care of her. Then there was college and my father's illness progressively getting worse. I lived at home for that, taking care of them. Then I went on the *American Voice*—magical—but he got progressively sicker during that. He passed away a few weeks ago. Since then, it's been all about taking care of my mother. She won't even get out of bed. Life just slips away so fast while you're busy focusing on everyone else."

Grant stayed stoically still, listening to her admissions. He was surprised to hear her opening up about her life to a near stranger, but it was almost like she wasn't talking to him. She was thinking out loud, and he just happened to be around to witness it. There was something haunted about the way she spoke, and for the first time in over a year, he had the urge to wrap his arms around this woman and kiss her.

It caught him off guard, so he stayed silent. His hand clutched the door handle as he contemplated her life, and how much she'd experienced at such a young age. He'd only just turned thirty-one years old, and yet, up until the last few years, his life had been smooth sailing. He'd never experienced a close death, massive heart break, or any sort of dramatic trauma.

Until now.

Every fiber of his being felt like it was falling apart in the wake of his own circumstances, but here was this young woman rising above all of it. She took everything in stride, taking care of those around her, while still managing to final in singing competitions and make a name for herself in the music industry.

"Sorry," she finally finished. "That's probably way more information than you wanted."

"It's okay." Grant reached one hand over and squeezed her forearm. Her skin seared him at the touch, but he didn't pull back.

She glanced down briefly at his hand on her arm, then her eyes flickered up to find his. The smallest hint of a smile passed her bright pink lips, and it warmed him.

CHAPTER FOUR

Simone parked at the top of the driveway beside a line of other expensive-as-hell cars in front of a giant house that had to have been in the many millions of dollars range.

"This house is gorgeous," he said, his eyes widening as he took in the sight.

Simone nodded. "Aria fell in love with it the moment she saw it. She and Ben have been living here about five years now. We used to do family dinners at my parents' house, but...with everything..."

She trailed off, and Grant didn't push her further. "Do you live around here?" he asked, changing the subject.

"I have a condo downtown," she replied with a shrug. "I'm more of a city gal."

He was, too, truthfully, though his house in New Zealand was on a cliff in the middle of nowhere. It hadn't been his choice to move there, but he loved the house none the same. Now in Los Angeles, he was staying at a fancy hotel downtown and enjoyed the view of the city below.

They climbed out of the car and she escorted him inside

where they found a group of people drinking cocktails in a gorgeous living room clearly designed by decorators.

Grant was beginning to feel like he didn't really fit into this lifestyle—luxury and glamor were not his foray. Especially now when he literally had nothing.

"Grant, this is Steele and her husband Xavier," Simone introduced him to a tall, heavily tattooed couple that looked perfect for one another. Xavier looked like he'd come right out of a boxing ring, and Steele looked like an older version of Simone. "They're long-time friends of the family."

"Good to meet you," he replied, shaking their hands.

"Grant is working on all the music for *Kiss Me, Kate*," Simone explained to them. "He just got here from New Zealand."

"Ah, that's where that accent is from," Steele replied. "It's good to meet you."

His accent wasn't particularly strong since he'd spent so much of his life traveling somewhere new every month, but admittedly he definitely had a light twang at the end that was all New Zealand. He rarely noticed it himself, but women loved to point it out.

Simone introduced him to the rest of the attendees, including her two sisters, their children, and a few other family friends who were also attending. Ben eventually joined them, apologizing for being late.

When they all sat down to dinner, the conversation went surprisingly well. As upscale as their lives seemed, the Reynoldses were genuinely down to earth and friendly people. Even if it was only for an hour or two, he was enjoying the escape from his problems back home and the constant worrying. Even more than that, though, he was enjoying getting to know Simone better.

He couldn't even remember the last time he'd really

paid attention to a woman or found himself constantly thinking of how beautiful she was. When she looked up from her plate and caught him watching her, her cheeks stained a gentle pink and he would have given anything to get a peek into her mind right then.

It was a mistake. He knew it was. Not only did he not have the time or space in his life for a romantic distraction right now, but the lead singer in the movie he was working on? She should be off limits. If something went wrong...

But despite the alarm bells in the back of his mind, he couldn't deny that he was attracted to Simone—the way her hair bounced when she moved, as if dancing alongside her laughter, or the way her brown eyes seemed to shine when she smiled. But as captivating as her beauty was, that wasn't the thing about her that snagged him and kept him from looking away.

It was the way the edges of her eyes didn't smile alongside her lips, like it was forced and for show. The way her fingers fidgeted in her lap, somehow restless and tired all at once. It was the way sadness seeped through every move she made and no one seemed to notice.

But he noticed. He noticed because that same sadness had taken up residence in his heart for months, and he knew the feeling better than any unwelcome guest.

Simone lifted her gaze to his from across the table, catching his attention for a moment longer than was necessary.

Grant smiled, and she responded in kind. Something told him that there might be a solution to both of their problems that was closer than they thought.

"When were you last in America, Grant?" Aria asked from across the table, clearly trying to draw him into the conversation.

He'd been keeping quiet, observing and listening to everyone else. "Last year, actually. I did a few months in New York collaborating on a new show's soundtrack."

"Oh, that's where I live!" Teagan spoke up from a few seats down. "Simone was back east staying with us last summer. I wonder if you two ever crossed paths."

Grant smiled, training his gaze on Simone. A blush crept up her cheeks, and it looked like she had just kicked Teagan under the table.

"I think I'd remember meeting her if we had," he replied. "Simone seems the type that's hard to forget."

Both Teagan and Aria looked at their youngest sister, huge smiles on their faces.

"You hear that, Simmy? You're hard to forget," Teagan teased.

"He's not wrong," Aria added.

"I-I definitely enjoyed New York," Simone said, stammering over her words a bit. "It's a great city."

Grant nodded. "I agree. It's on my list of places to live one day."

"You want to leave New Zealand?" Aria asked. "I've only ever heard amazing things about that country."

"I'm never home for more than a few weeks at a time, so it only makes sense that I move out this way. Most of my work is here in Los Angeles or New York or London." Grant pushed the food around his plate as he tried to consider where he actually thought of as *home*. New Zealand had his parents and a few friends, but still...it wasn't home. Home was a feeling—one he hadn't experienced in quite some time.

"I've potentially got a project in London later this year," Simone mused. "I might be doing a collaboration with Lily

Allen on this new record she's working on. Still waiting to see if that actually happens."

Grant lifted his brows. "Wow...she's amazing. That would be an incredible opportunity."

Simone's eyes lit up for the first time since they'd met, passion flowing through her irises as she continued to talk about the opportunity and more. The sadness that normally dwelled in her expression was completely gone as he listened to her, and he recognized that artistic excitement.

He wanted to feel that again—that strength and vigor that came with a project he couldn't wait to get his hands on. *Kiss Me, Kate* was fun, but it was a reprisal. It wasn't new, it wasn't *him*. He needed to find his excitement again, and something told him that this woman was just the person to inspire him.

CHAPTER FIVE

Simone stared in the bathroom mirror, her hands firmly planted on the counter as she leaned closer to the glass. She didn't know what she was looking for, but hell...the way Grant had stared at her during dinner had made her entire body ignite in flames.

Gazing at her reflection now, she couldn't pinpoint what he had seen. She couldn't see what made him not turn away from her nearly once for the entire hour-long meal. At first, she'd felt flattered by the attention, but there was something about his eyes that didn't brag or praise. There was a kinship, and somehow his very eyes alone seemed to see right through her, as if her defenses were sheer.

She sighed, finally washing her hands and shaking the thoughts from her head. She shouldn't have opened up to him as much as she had on the drive over. It was unusual for her to share so much of herself with anyone, let alone someone who was mostly a stranger. He didn't know her life. No one did. Her family kept secrets tighter than a military fort, and being the youngest child, she was always the 'good' one. She never caused waves, she always took care of her parents, and she never got in anyone's way.

It was probably why she dressed the way she did or covered her body in ink. They were small rebellions that made her unique—gave her a voice.

Simone dried her hands on the soft towel next to the sink, then fluffed her fingers through her hair. She didn't want to think about all of this today, and she didn't want to dwell on the handsome foreigner who made her body tighten with just a look.

Clearly, it had been too long since she'd had sex and it was wreaking havoc on her judgment.

Swinging open the bathroom door, she stepped out into the hallway and almost slammed right into a tall, broad chest. "Oh!" she startled, her hands against his muscled pecs to catch herself. "Sorry. I...um...sorry."

The edges of Grant's lips turned north, but it wasn't a full smile. Closer to a smirk, almost, but somehow just as warm. "I was just looking for you," he replied. "Would you mind giving me a ride back to my hotel?"

"Of course not. I'm the one who brought you here, so it's only right. Right for me to go home with you, I mean. Wait, no, I mean, to take you home." She wanted to die, but she couldn't stop from rambling. "Let's...let's go. My car's out front. Well, you know where it is since I drove you here."

Grant placed his hands on her upper arms and held her still. "Breathe."

Nerves jittered across her skin, but she did as he instructed and took a deep breath. Her body instantly seemed to relax under his hold, and the need to ramble dissipated. However, another need quickly took its place. The way he stood so close to her, his face inches from hers and his hands gripping her arms...she was reminded for the second time of just how long it'd been since she'd been in such close proximity to a man.

"Better," he replied, smiling wider this time. "Come on. Traffic should be lighter by now."

She chuckled, still trying to ignore her previous line of thinking. "There's no such thing in Los Angeles."

Sure enough, thirty minutes later and they were sitting in nearly standstill traffic into downtown. They inched along in silence, and Simone tried to think of something to say, but nothing came to mind. Every thought she had was leading back to one thing, and she suddenly felt like a teenager in heat.

Her eyes flickered sideways to him for a moment. Maybe she should just put the car into park, crawl into his lap, and fuck his brains out. Get it entirely out of her system.

The idea was too insane, even for her.

But still...there was something to be said for giving in for a brief moment. Maybe then they could actually work together without her body internally combusting every time he was near her. She barely knew him at all, and yet her body seemed to have already made its decision.

Simone took a deep breath. "So, are you planning on doing any sightseeing while you're here?" she broke the silence with a rudimentary question. Anything to get them talking about something other than how badly she wanted to taste his lips or feel his hands on her again.

"I haven't really thought about it," he replied. "I've been to America dozens of times before. Seen quite a lot. Really, I'm just here for the job."

"Right. Focus on work." she replied awkwardly, her hands gripping the steering wheel as she pulled them off the highway and toward his hotel. "Always a good thing."

"I don't know if I agree with that." Grant shifted in his seat so that he was facing her more. "There's something to be said for...distractions."

"Is there?" She tucked a strand of hair behind her ear, but it promptly fell out again.

Grant reached over and tucked the same strand of hair behind her ear, and this time it stayed. "There is. Distractions are good for the soul. Good for one's sanity."

She wanted to turn to look at him, but she kept her gaze to the street. "I...I don't feel very sane," she admitted, a slight tease in her voice.

Am I flirting? If so, she was sure doing a terrible job.

He smiled at her then pointed to a building on their right. "That's my hotel. You can pull into the garage right there and find a parking spot."

"I could just drop you off at the front."

"You could," he replied. "But if you parked, then you could come up and be distracted for a little while."

Simone's eyes cut sideways to look at him. His face was completely serious, his eyes practically boring holes into her. "Distractions are good for the soul," she repeated his earlier words.

Grant smiled. "There's a fully stocked minibar..."

"Ah, the key to a woman's heart," she kidded, pulling the car into the parking garage and searching for a spot. "I guess I could be tempted with one drink. Just to relax."

"Sure. Just to relax."

Or something like that...

CHAPTER SIX

Simone parked, and the duo climbed out of the car and headed for the garage elevators up into the hotel. Grant pressed the button and they stood side by side, waiting for the doors to open.

In that moment, the garage was so hushed Simone would probably have heard a pin drop. She wasn't sure what to say...hell, she wasn't sure what she had agreed to. All she knew was that her entire body was tense and pulsing and she wanted him to be the one to put out the fire he'd sparked.

The doors finally slid open, and they stepped onto the elevator car. He pressed another button for the very top floor, swiping a hotel card past the security light.

"Penthouse?" Simone turned to him, one brow raised. "You didn't mention you had the entire top floor."

"Ben's studio is very generous," he replied, shrugging his shoulders like it was nothing.

She doubted that it was all the studio, but she didn't ask further. The elevator doors slowly slid closed, the parking garage disappearing from view behind them.

"Simone?" Grant turned to face her, taking a step closer.

She lifted her eyes to him, angling her body to face his. "Yes?"

He moved even closer, barely inches from her now. Her chest rose and fell faster with each breath at his proximity. "I've been thinking about kissing you all night."

She swallowed hard but didn't respond. *Yes, please.*

"I don't think I can wait much longer," he continued, his voice lower and raspier now, like gravel scraping against her in a way that made her entire body shiver.

She breathed out in one long exhale. "Don't wait..."

His lips were on hers immediately, as he stepped into her body so she had to back up against the elevator wall. He placed a hand on the surface of the wall on either side of her, pinning her between his arms as his lips slid over hers.

Frenzied, tugging—his mouth smashed against hers until she lost every breath in her lungs. Gasping, she parted for him and his tongue quickly found hers. It was the most hurried, need-filled kiss she'd ever experienced in her life. Like they couldn't get enough of each other. Couldn't stop— didn't want to stop. He tasted her like he wanted to devour her, and her body ignited beneath him.

Her hips arched towards his, pressing against him as he pushed her farther back against the elevator wall. She could already feel his length between them, startlingly large and hard against her belly.

A dinging sound caught her attention, her eyes opening to see the elevator doors sliding apart. "We're here," she mumbled against his lips.

He growled, gripping her hips with both hands and lifting her against him. She instinctively wrapped her legs around his waist as he held her and walked them off the elevator. His mouth was on her neck, sucking and nibbling, and all she wanted to do was throw her head back and give him every inch of herself.

The room came into perspective around her—a large hotel living room with impeccable modern furniture in front of entire walls of glass windows that looked out onto Los Angeles below. There was a kitchen to one side, but they bypassed it entirely as he headed for a back hallway.

Simone's skin danced with nerves as he carried her, presumably, to the bedroom. She wanted to find a reason not to do this—to run out of here right now and not let her body call the shots.

But it was too late.

Excitement tore through every cell in her body as she writhed against him, wanting more...wanting him.

"Oh, God..." She gasped as he found the perfect spot right below her ear that always made her shiver.

His knees hit the edge of the giant king-sized bed first, but he crawled onto the mattress and laid her back against the comforter. Her knees were still locked around his waist as he pressed down against her, kissing her once more.

"Fuck...I love kissing you," he groaned against her mouth, his hands roaming the rest of her body below. He gripped the bottom hem of her dress and began pushing it up the length of her body.

Simone wiggled with him, helping him slide it over her head before he tossed the dress onto the floor. In just a bra and panties, she felt the cool air tingling against her skin for only a moment before his body covered hers again.

She ran her hands down the front of his chest, finding each button on his shirt and making quick work of undoing them before she pushed the fabric off his shoulders and let it fall to the bed beside them.

They continued kissing, feasting on one another as her

hands explored every rigid inch of his perfectly sculpted body. Hell, she'd known he was fit just from looking at him, but his clothes had hidden just how muscular he truly was. His stomach was a ridged terrain of abs and a perfect V pointing down toward his jeans, which was her next mission to remove. She began undoing the button but couldn't get it to work for some reason.

Grant quickly leaned backward and unfastened them himself, shoving the jeans down his legs and kicking them off the edge of the bed. Tight briefs covered his bulging package but did nothing to hide exactly how large and ready he was.

She squirmed as she watched him, wanting every inch he had to offer. Reaching behind her own body, she unfastened her bra and then tossed that off, pulling her panties down her legs last.

His eyes flamed as he watched her and then quickly removed his own briefs. Both entirely naked, he pressed her back into the mattress as his hands found her breasts while he kissed her. Smart, delicate movements, he manipulated her nipples, cupping the weight of her breasts in his hands as she arched against him, wanting more. He kissed down her jaw line, trailing down her neck to her collarbone, until he took her nipple between his lips. His tongue flicked over the tip.

"Ah!" Her body jumped at the sensation, both eager for more and already feeling pushed past the breaking point.

His teeth grazed her, her breath catching as he made steady work of sucking and nibbling and devouring her breasts until she was certain she was ready to come from that alone.

"These are perfect," he said, the sound vibrating against her skin. "Absolutely fucking perfect."

Nerves began to swell up in her belly at his compliment. It was so affectionate...so hungry...so full of emotion and want. "Grant..."

"Mmm..." He hummed against her skin.

Simone pushed against his shoulders lightly. "Grant, wait..."

His gaze slid up to hers, hovering over her but keeping his weight off of her. "You okay?"

She swallowed hard. "Yeah...more than okay, but..."

Grant moved to the side, stretching out across the bed next to her. "But?"

"I don't do this," she said, her fingers fidgeting with the blanket beneath them. "I don't just jump into bed with different men every night. I don't want you thinking that about me."

He smiled and shook his head. "I definitely don't think you're like that, Simone."

She pushed up on her elbows, turning to look at him. "Really? Because we just met and I'm naked in your bed."

His tongue slid over his bottom lip as his gaze grazed across her body. "I'm *fully* aware." He cleared his throat. "We don't have to do anything, but I definitely don't see you as one of those women. Simone, you've had to deal with more than I've ever experienced in my life. Just based on the little bit you told me earlier about yourself, your entire life revolves around other people. Seeing this side of you? The side that throws caution to the wind and just does what *you* want? That's a damn relief. Everyone needs those escapes."

"The *distractions*?" she teased, turning on to her side and tracing her fingers across the muscular line that crossed his hip bone and dipped lower.

Grant growled lightly. "What do you want tonight,

Simone? Think about just you. Just your wants. Tell me, and I'll do it."

Her breath quickened as different desires crossed her mind, begging her to put herself first just this once...just this once. She wanted to dive in, take for her own pleasure. She wanted him. "I want this..." she finally responded, her voice breathy and low.

"Specifically, Simone." His eyes flared, a tiny smile grew at the corners of his lips. "Tell me..."

She knew exactly what she wanted, but asking for it? That was something she'd never done before. Simone cleared her throat, leaning her body into his. "I want...I want your mouth."

Grant brushed his lips past her cheek, moving to her ear. "Where do you want my mouth?" he whispered, gruff and heady.

He kissed down the line of her neck, his tongue sliding against her skin. Her body writhed forward, fire swirling in her belly at the sensation. "Where, Simone..."

She swallowed hard, taking a deep breath. "Between my legs."

Grant smiled and pushed forward against her, laying her back on the bed before he moved down the length of her body. Her knees were driven apart as he settled between them, his lips on her stomach and then her hip bone...and then her thigh. His tongue slid across the skin on her inner thigh, sending a trembling wave through her as he got closer and closer to her core. In slow, taunting circles, he moved closer and then he was there. His tongue flicking across her core and her clit as she her back arched off the bed at the contact.

"Oh!" She gasped but her hips pushed forward, wanting more.

Long, slow licks mixed with short, teasing circles around her clit made her entire body shake with every sensation rolling over her. Every worry that usually plagued her mind—her parents, her responsibilities, her career—all of it disappeared as for these few minutes she focused on one thing—pleasure.

The decadence of being purely selfish was something she hadn't tasted in years, and here was an almost stranger, demanding she give it a try. Damn, she was glad she did.

When her climax hit, she nearly catapulted off the bed, but Grant gripped her hips and held her to him as he licked and sucked until her body finally quieted.

"God, you come hard when you let go," he said, a huskiness to his voice that made her skin prick with excitement. He climbed back up her body, pressing her down into the mattress with the heaviness of his own muscular frame.

His lips were on hers again when she reached between them, wrapping her hand around his length. Thick and hard, he swelled against her palm as she stroked him. Despite her recent release, the tension was already building inside her again, and this time, she wanted him.

Grant groaned, his forehead to hers, then slid his hand between her legs, finding her clit once more. He ran his finger in circles over her, pushing her closer and closer to the edge again as their lips warred with one another. Fast and forceful, they kissed like they were fighting.

He reached into the nightstand drawer beside the bed and pulled out a small foil packet. Soft crinkling joined the sound of her heavy breathing as he unwrapped the condom. Then he slid it over his dick and positioned himself at her entrance. She thrust her hips toward him, wanting it now, but he pulled back.

"Eager?" The corner of his lips turned up in a grin.

Simone swallowed, her breathing heavy as her chest rose and fell with anticipation. "Yes..."

He thrust inside with zero hesitation, zero warning, and it was everything she'd hoped it would be and more.

"Grant!" She gasped his name as her body trembled against his, working to accommodate the sheer size of him. Splintering stars burst behind her eyelids as every glorious thrust brought her closer and closer to spiraling over the edge.

"God, yes..." Grant kissed her neck, nipping her flesh. "You're so fucking tight around me." He stilled for a moment as they both adjusted to the filling sensations. Her entire body felt ready to tip over the edge at that alone, but she held back, wanting it to last. She wanted to feel him inside her again and again, each thrust more powerful than the next.

She couldn't even believe she was here, or what she was doing. It was so unlike everything she was, and yet, there was something about this moment that felt completely right. That felt like *her*. That felt like this was who she'd been all along if only she hadn't been denying herself for years.

Her next orgasm hit her without warning, suddenly knocking her into the shattered abyss as he thrust into her harder, deeper, faster. Then he was coming next, holding himself as deep as possible, grunting against her neck as they were pinned together so tight.

When she could finally catch her breath again, Grant slid to the side and dropped to his back on the mattress beside her. She stared up at the ceiling, their legs still tangled together, just trying to find her breath and calm her racing pulse.

"That was fucking incredible." Grant finally broke the silence.

"Mmm," she agreed. "Amazing."

Despite every desire to stay immobile in bed, Simone forced herself to her feet and headed to the bathroom. Once she was all cleaned up, she stared at her naked body in the mirror. Tattoos splattered her rib cage, arm, and shoulder, but now there were small red marks and bites across her neck and breasts, too. She smiled at the recent memory and headed back into the bedroom.

Grant was still stretched out on the bed, his eyes closed.

"I should probably get going," Simone said, grabbing her dress off the carpet.

"What?" Grant opened his eyes, confusion on his face.

"Just saying goodbye," she continued, nerves now swarming inside her as the awkwardness settled in.

He was still practically a stranger, and this was clearly a one-night stand—something she'd never done before. She wasn't sure what the etiquette was, but she knew enough about men to know that when the deed was done, it was time to go.

Grant leaned across the bed and pulled her dress from her hands, tossing it onto the floor on the other side of the room. "Get your cute little ass back in this bed, Simone."

She chuckled. "Round two already?"

"Mmm...maybe later." Grant pulled the sheets down and climbed under them, gesturing for her to join him. "But first, we're going to cuddle."

"You want to cuddle?" That was new.

She climbed under the sheets next to him, letting him wrap himself around her and pull her to his chest.

Grant kissed her cheek. "Yep, all night."

Simone smiled and closed her eyes, but she wasn't sure whether she was touched at the sweetness of his gesture or if she was terrified at the intimacy of the moment. His arms wrapped around her, his soft breathing in her ear as he fell asleep...it was so vulnerable, so personal, so...real.

Simone wasn't the girl to have a one-night stand, but she also hadn't ever been long-term either. And Grant? Well, she didn't know who the hell he was.

CHAPTER SEVEN

GRANT OPENED his eyes the next morning and turned to look at Simone. Instead, he found rustled sheets and an empty bed. Frowning, he sat up and glanced around the room. Sure enough, her shoes and dress were gone.

Sighing, he climbed out of bed and headed for the bathroom. Turning on the faucet, he set the water to hot before he got in and began washing. He honestly wasn't sure why he was bothered by the fact that she had left. It had very clearly been a casual exchange, a spur-of-the-moment decision led purely by physical desire.

And yet...that wasn't true. He was interested in a lot more about Simone than just her fantastic body. Hell, just thinking about her body made him hard again. He gripped his length, sliding his hand up and down slowly.

The way she'd writhed beneath him, panting, calling his name...it was one of the hottest things he'd ever seen. He'd had his share of women—though he'd never been the manwhore type—and yet, there was something about Simone's pouty lips, her fire-filled eyes, that made him crazy with need. Having sex with her should have gotten it out of his system, but he was even more ready to go now than he had been last night.

Grant pumped harder, groaning at the images from last night that flitted through his mind until he finally released. "Fuck..."

Quickly, he cleaned up and finished his shower, climbing out and drying off with a thick, hotel towel. He made a call down to room service, ordering some breakfast, and then checked his cell phone.

An unknown number had texted him, the notification popping up across the screen. *Thanks for last night ;)*

Grant smiled and tapped back a quick reply. *I'd rather be thanking you in person for this morning, but you're not here.*

He waited a moment, watching for the bubble to appear that indicated she was typing a response back. None came. Sighing, he placed his phone back down and finished getting dressed. He had a lot of work to do today anyway, so he wasn't going to focus on the vixen who'd rocked his world and then left him high and dry the next morning.

A knock came at the door of his suite at the same moment his phone rang.

"Hello?" Grant answered the phone as he walked toward his hotel door.

"Grant, it's Andrew. We've got a lead."

Grant sighed, never loving the conversations with his lawyer. Even if it was good news, it was still just honey on a pile of shit. "What's the lead?" He opened the door, letting room service in. The attendant moved quickly with a courteous nod, setting up breakfast on the dining table for him.

"She's using a pseudonym, and apparently that name was last seen on a flight to New York."

He tipped the attendant as the young man left, closing

the door behind him. "She's in America?"

"Potentially." His lawyer sighed. "But there's a downside to this. It doesn't look like she's spending any of the money. We can't prove that she's the one who embezzled everything unless she's caught with the cash."

Fuck. "And until that happens, it looks like I took everything."

"Exactly. Don't plan on touching down in New Zealand anytime soon."

He had no plans to return to someplace where his arrest warrant was ready and waiting for him. What a goddamn mess. It was one thing that the woman he loved ran off with his best friend. That alone had broken his heart into a million pieces. But she'd also wiped their accounts cleaned, embezzled from the composer's association he was the chairman of, along with several other boards they were on, and left enough evidence behind to point the finger at him.

"How are you getting me out of this, Andrew?" Grant asked. "I finish up my current project within a month."

"You're flying to London next, right? You'll be fine there while we sort this out."

Grant shook his head, even though Andrew couldn't see him. "I am, but I can't just never go home. I still have my parents there."

"Fly them out to London with you. You're getting decent paychecks from these jobs."

It wasn't the same. Sure, he was comfortable with money, but he'd still lost everything he'd been saving for a future. Though, it wasn't really relevant anymore since the future he'd planned for was already gone.

"Just do me a favor, Grant," Andrew continued. "Keep your head down at work and focus on that. Don't stir up any waves over there. No women, no parties, no—"

"Fun?" Grant finished for him. "You want me to just stay a hermit? Hard pass."

"I'm serious, Grant. As stupid as it may sound, you have enough heat on your name that anything else on top of it would just be a disaster. Stay out of the spotlight. Stay out of trouble. And whatever you do, stay the fuck away from Serena."

Like he had any plans on ever seeing his ex-wife again. "She's not coming here, so don't worry. I want nothing to do with her."

"Good. I've got to go, but I'll keep you apprised of any developments." With that, Andrew hung up the phone.

Grant sat down to eat his breakfast, tossing his phone onto the table beside him. His lawyer didn't need to worry. He had zero plans for causing waves. Hell, he'd never been one to get in trouble before he'd met Serena anyway, but she was a whirlwind of a woman who'd come into his life as quickly as she'd left. They'd only been married a short time, and he was so sure he'd been in love with her but looking back...it was infatuation. It was lust, and maybe a little excitement. She was a daredevil who pushed the limits and pushed him out of his comfort zone as often as she could.

But the brakes were on now. She'd left him enough of a mess to clean up that he wasn't about to go make more of his own now. His thoughts flickered back to last night—Simone. Seeing her would be messy. Hell, it could jeopardize this entire job if things ended badly.

Grant took another bite of his eggs and thought it over. He couldn't afford the fall out—financially or personally—if things with Simone went south. Not right now. Not when things were so tense in his life.

Whatever they'd had, he was leaving it behind in last night.

CHAPTER EIGHT

"You're still off-key and butchering this line," Grant said, staring Simone down from where he was sitting at the piano to one side of the set.

Simone clenched her jaw, already irritated at the nonstop criticism he'd had the entire rehearsal so far. Since the moment she'd gotten onto set this morning, he'd been either ignoring her completely or negatively commenting on her performance. This movie was being shot like one live play, and so there were no do-overs or second chances. She knew she had to get it right, but that didn't mean she was failing that badly. Hell, she was pretty damn good.

She shifted her weight onto one foot and glared at him. "Maybe *you* can do better, then?"

"I'm not the singer, sweetheart," he replied. "But I don't need you destroying my melodies."

Simone turned to the director. "I need to take five."

Mario Cruz gave her a small nod. "That's probably a good idea. It's actually getting kind of late in the day. Let's call it a wrap until tomorrow."

Simone was immediately relieved. Honestly, she wasn't sure what the hell Grant's problem was today. They'd had an amazing night last night, and she really hadn't thought it would affect them working together.

Clearly, she had been wrong.

Taking off for her trailer, Simone wanted nothing more than to pour herself a nice glass of red wine and get lost in some trashy reality television. Despite her annoyance with the genre as a whole, she had to admit that it was incredibly entertaining to watch housewives' petty squabbles or anything Kardashian.

"Simone," a voice called out behind her.

She recognized it immediately but kept walking. There was nothing she wanted to hear from Grant right now, and after his tirade of insults all day, she wasn't gearing up for any more. The trailer door handle was cool beneath her palm as she grabbed it and pulled. She stepped inside and reached to close the door behind her. His hand on the door-frame blocked her way.

"Move your hand or it's getting crushed," she commanded through narrow eyes.

"Christ," Grant replied, moving his hand out of the way but stepping closer to block the door with his entire body now. "That seems a little harsh."

"*I'm* harsh?" Simone scoffed. "Have you seen yourself today? You've been an asshole from minute one."

Grant shrugged his shoulders, pushing his hands into his pockets. "I've been a bit of a pill."

Simone crossed her arms over her chest, surveying him for a moment. There was a look of remorse on his face that did seem sincere, but she still didn't know him well enough to believe it. She might have jumped into bed with him, but today had reminded her exactly how little she knew this man.

Grant stepped forward and closed the trailer door behind him. She did her best not to notice the way his jaw tensed, perfectly covered with a hint of stubble, or the way his arms were filling out his T-shirt sleeves, stretched tight around his muscular biceps.

"I was honestly ticked off when I woke up to you gone this morning," Grant continued. "I thought we'd had a pretty good night together, and that...I don't know. It stung."

She blinked, confused. "You...wait...that upset you? I was doing you a favor."

Now he seemed to be the one confused. "What favor?"

Simone stepped to the side, leaning against the small kitchen counter to one wall of the trailer. "You know. Guys always want the girl to leave after a one-night stand. I just made it less awkward because you didn't have to tell me to go."

Grant's head tipped back and he laughed...loud.

She startled at first, but then irritation flooded her. "What's so funny?"

"We're not in college, Simone. This isn't a frat house. I wasn't trying to fuck you to add another conquest to my list," he said, closing the gap between them as he walked over to her. He took her hand in his, squeezing gently. "We're two grown adults who wanted to spend time together. I wanted to spend time with you."

"Oh." She honestly didn't know what to say to that. Everything about what they'd done had screamed one-night-stand, but now...she wasn't so sure. "So, you want...you wanted this to be more?"

He shrugged his shoulders. "Well, I still leave for

London in a month, but...yeah, I want more. Since the moment I met you, I've been interested in you, Simone. You're gorgeous and witty and have a fiery temper that gives me life. Maybe it's crazy, maybe it's fast, but if there's one thing I've learned lately, it's that the good times don't last. We have to enjoy life while we can, and next to you...life has been pretty enjoyable. I can only imagine another month of that would be even better."

She'd never gone into anything before with an expiration date. Honestly, that sounded fucking terrible. What if she really fell for him and then had to say goodbye? She wasn't sure she had the emotional stamina to deal with that kind of roller coaster.

But at the same time, he was right. She did really enjoy his company, and she'd been infatuated with him from the moment he first pissed her off on set days ago. There was no doubt in her mind that she'd regret not experiencing this next month with him...even if that was all they had.

"I've never done anything like that before...so casual."

Grant lifted her hand to his lips and kissed her knuckles. "It seems to me there's a lot of things you've never done... maybe it's time we changed that."

He wasn't wrong there. She'd lived so much of her life swimming in the shallow end of the pool and lifeguarding for everyone around her. She'd never taken real risks or put herself first, and here she was, contemplating diving into something that would undoubtedly end in heartbreak.

Fuck it.

"Okay," she said. "One month. Casual. Just fun."

A smile spread across Grant's face. "I want to take you somewhere tonight. It'll be a surprise. Text me your address and be ready to go at eight."

Simone nibbled on her bottom lip but nodded her head. Based on the way her stomach somersaulted when he was around, she had no doubt that this was going to be one of the most exhilarating months of her life.

Until it all crashed and burned.

CHAPTER NINE

"I DON'T THINK I've been to this part of town before." Simone stepped out of the passenger seat of Grant's rental car.

He circled the car and reached a hand toward her. "I think you'll like it."

She took his hand tentatively, surprised at the sweet gesture. He squeezed the tips of her fingers between his, and butterflies swirled in her stomach. They passed several storefronts, then a restaurant, then a bar, but continued walking down the sidewalk. Simone frowned, wondering how far they were going when they'd already passed several really nice date-worthy places.

They reached the corner and turned down a dark alleyway.

"There's nothing down here, Grant," she said, slowing her steps.

He chuckled. "See that blue light?"

A small blue lightbulb hung from a chain next to a dark, metal door at the end of the alleyway. No signs, no indication that it led to anything at all.

"That's where we're going."

They approached the door, and he knocked on it three times.

Nothing happened.

"Maybe it's closed?" Simone glanced back the way they'd come. "Probably not a lot of people hanging out at the end of dark alleyways who aren't murderers."

He knocked three more times. "Have a little faith."

With a creaky squeak, the metal door swung open. They had to jump back quickly so as not to be hit by it.

"IDs?" A man in a white shirt and suspenders with a handlebar mustache was bathed in the blue light as he stood in the doorway staring at them.

They each pulled out their driver's licenses, and he examined them against a list on aged parchment paper.

"Head on in."

"Thanks," Grant replied, taking her hand and leading them past the doorman. The light was even darker in the hallway, but a red light glowed at the end, peeking out from between two thick, velvet curtains that she saw as they got closer.

Grant pushed aside one set of curtains and held it open for her.

Simone stepped through and was immediately shocked at the venue they'd just entered. Warm wood tones on the paneled walls, plank floor, and beamed ceilings completely encapsulated the large room. Red velvet booths ran along on wall, and on the opposite wall was a long stone bar where people were seated, engaged in lively conversation with bartenders in old-timey clothes.

"Is this a speakeasy?" She turned to look at Grant as he wrapped an arm around her waist.

He nodded. "I came across it a few years back on one of

my trips here. Now I come anytime I'm in Los Angeles. You won't find a single mention of this place online. No signs. No anything. The only way to find out about it is from other patrons."

"I feel like I should be in a flapper's dress, or something like that," she teased, following his lead as he guided them to a booth in the back.

"Nah," he replied, steering her toward the booths. "Everyone here is nicely dressed, and they only do the themed nights on Fridays and Saturdays."

Too bad it was Thursday. "We should come back tomorrow then! Dress the full nine yards," she suggested.

He laughed. "We could."

They slid into a booth, and a bartender showed up in seconds, placing two glasses in front of them—one a small rocks glass and the other a champagne flute. Simone eyed the two different glasses after the bartender left. "What are these?"

"Mine's an old fashioned," Grant said, gesturing to the rocks glass. "Yours is a French 75. Both popular drinks from the 1920's."

"And they just automatically pick a drink for you?" That seemed odd, to be honest.

"Try it," he assured her. "They never get it wrong."

Simone took a sip from her flute, the sweetness of the champagne and sugar mixing perfectly with the acidity of the lemon juice. "Mmm. This is actually exactly what I would have ordered."

"See? They know what they're doing." Grant took a swallow from his glass, a small moan parting his lips.

Tension built in Simone's belly at the very sound of his pleasure. She scooted closer to him on the round booth bench, leaning into his side as he wrapped an arm around her shoulders. "Thanks for bringing me here. I've always wanted to experience something like this."

He lifted his glass to hers. "To trying new things."

She clinked the edge of her flute to his glass. "To being bold and baring it all."

Grant lifted one brow. "I would love to see you bare it all."

She blushed at his implications. "I'm sure you would, but that's not what I meant."

"I'll be good. For now," he teased, his fingers drawing small circles on her upper arm. "Tell me something about you I don't know, Simone."

"Hmm...there's a lot about me you don't know."

"Pick one thing."

Simone considered her options. She honestly wasn't the type to open up and share much about herself at all. She was always focused on other people, but something about Grant made her not want to answer trivially. Sure, she could tell him her favorite color or something silly like that, but there was nothing light or trivial about Grant. He was heavy and serious in all of the best ways. He overwhelmed her, and she loved every moment of it.

"When I was in college, I originally planned to be a doctor," she began. "But...I couldn't pass my pre-med courses and one of my teachers told me that I should pick something different because I'd never be successful in medicine. I ended up getting a fine arts degree and pursuing music instead, but I always felt like I failed and just fell back on the next best thing."

Grant sighed softly. "You think being a singer was you settling?"

She nodded slightly. "I don't know, honestly. I love singing. It's my passion. But...it's not really a 'job.'"

"We live in a world that doesn't value the arts as a career or a serious life path," Grant replied. "When I told my parents I was going to write music for a living, they never took me seriously. They kept waiting for me to go out and get a 'real job.' There are people who are meant to be doctors and lawyers and accountants, whose talents lie in healing, and facts and numbers and solving problems. Then there are people like us, whose talents lie in creating problems, stirring up emotions, building melodies and lyrics that tear down defenses and overwhelm the senses. We could be the fixers, we could be the solvers, but, damn...it feels so good to make something brand new, to tear it all down and make a fucking mess."

"Wow." Simone considered what he was saying for a moment. "I never really thought about it like that. Music has always been what I've loved, but I never really believed it could be a career. Or rather, that it *should*."

"Yet here you are, doing it." Grant took another sip of his drink. "And succeeding on top of all that."

She felt her cheeks warm slightly at the compliment. "When I was on stage in the finals at *American Voice*...God, this is embarrassing."

"What? Tell me."

"There was a girl in the front row and she was crying when I sang. There were a few people I could see crying—the stage lights were so bright though—but she was *crying*. Full on sobbing." Simone pulled her lips between her teeth for a moment, biting them before releasing. "And it was exhilarating. I was thrilled that she was breaking down... because of me. My words, my sound, my voice did that. Is that sick?"

He shook his head. "No. It's beautiful. Broken is beautiful."

They were quiet for a moment. Simone leaned closer to him, tucking her head into his neck. "Sometimes I feel broken."

"All the time," he replied. "you are beautiful."

She hummed lightly, happiness swirling in her chest, which might have had something to do with the alcohol but definitely had everything to do with the man beside her. He angled his face to hers, those deep green eyes piercing her for a moment too long so that it almost hurt.

When his lips touched hers and his tongue slid into her mouth, there was the hint of sugar and bitterness, perfectly blended. She moaned slightly, running her hand up his chest to behind his neck. She held him against her, kissing both soft and hard as their lips warred.

The way he kissed her was hungry...needy...filling. It was unlike anything she'd ever experienced before. His arm slipped around her waist and pulled her closer to him. There was a heat between them that made her feel dizzy, the scene around them falling away as her attention was only focused on his lips, his tongue...him.

Music suddenly filled the room—much louder than the soft overhead serenades that had been previously playing. Pulling apart, they looked toward the source to see a group of musicians in the far corner playing big band music and a trio of couples swing dancing on the dance floor.

"Oh my gosh," Simone said, immediately captivated by the movements and atmosphere as the dancers flipped and swung across the floor like they'd been doing it their whole lives. "This couldn't be more perfect."

"One of my favorite things about this place," Grant admitted, settling back against the booth to watch the show. "I'm not terrible on the dance floor, but these guys...they're fucking amazing."

She nodded. "They are. I've always loved big band music. The old soul in me."

He gently pushed her hair behind her shoulder, caressing her neck softly with his fingertips. "I like your soul. It's the first thing I noticed about you when you were tumbling down from the ceiling."

"I was *not* tumbling. More like a graceful descent."

"A graceful descent into cracking your head open on the concrete floor, sure."

Simone laughed. "Well, thankfully, someone caught me."

"Sounds like a hero," he teased. "You should really give him an award. Maybe the key to the city."

Simone laughed, laying her head against his shoulder as they continued to watch the show. For her first night of making herself a priority and getting out there, she had to admit...she was enjoying it so much more than she thought she would. She hadn't considered her responsibilities once. She just felt...happy. Relaxed. Life felt easy.

Maybe this was how it was always supposed to have felt.

CHAPTER TEN

"Mom?" Simone gently tapped on the bedroom door at her parents' house. "Are you in here?"

"Yeah," a muted response came back.

Simone pushed the door open wider to see her mother's figure lying in bed, the blankets pulled high up over her shoulders. She sighed at the sight, an ache in her heart at the thought that her mother, Betty, was still in bed in the late afternoon on a Monday.

It wasn't that unusual. Hell, this was their new normal in more ways than one. Simone had stayed at her parents' house for almost a month after her father's passing, and her mother had spent most of that time in bed. Since moving back into her apartment, though, she hadn't been around as much. She still tried to make it over every other day, but when she did, her mother's improvement only seemed minimally better.

"Have you eaten today, Mom?" she asked, sitting on the edge of the bed and rubbing her mother's back.

Her mother stirred, turning toward her and giving her a small smile. "I think I forgot. What time is it?"

"Almost four," Simone replied. "How about I cook us something for dinner?"

Betty sat up, yawning and rubbing her eyes. "That would be nice, dear. I probably should eat something."

"Have you been out of bed today?"

Betty nodded. "I was at the cemetery first thing this morning like always. I never miss a morning with your father."

Simone squeezed her mother's hand, knowing full well that her mother would probably continue to visit Jack's grave every day for the rest of her life. "Well, I'm glad you're getting out of the house."

"I'm not sure there's any food in the house to cook," her mother admitted, sliding her legs off the edge of the bed before standing up. "I haven't been to the store in a while."

She actually hadn't been to the store in months. "I brought over groceries," Simone told her. "There's plenty for at least the next week. I also stopped at the pharmacy and picked up your medications. They're in the bathroom vanity."

"You're so good to me," her mother replied, gently touching the side of Simone's face. "You do so much for me."

"Don't worry about it, Mom," Simone assured her. "It's really no problem."

They headed down toward the kitchen where Simone began taking out ingredients to make a stir-fry. Her mother sat at the breakfast counter and sipped on a glass of red wine.

"Mom, what do you think about going through Dad's clothes this weekend? Maybe donating some of them?" Simone asked. "I think it would be good to clean out his closet and start to put his things away. The house still looks like he lives here."

"He does live here, Simmy." Her mother didn't lift her eyes from her glass, pouring herself a second. "I can't get rid of his things."

"Not 'get rid of.' Just donate. I think it makes you sadder to see his suits every day, don't you?"

Her mother shook her head. "No. It's comforting. It's only been a few weeks, Simmy. I'm not ready yet."

"Okay," Simone acquiesced. She certainly wasn't going to force her mother into anything she wasn't ready for, but she felt the need to do *something*. "What about the memorial coming up? Anything else you need help with?"

The memorial was planned for the one-month anniversary of her father's passing. They hadn't wanted it to be too soon, giving all the extended family and friends time to coordinate their travel.

"No," she replied. "You all have already taken care of everything. It's going to be a beautiful day."

Simone was both looking forward to it and dreading it at the same time. She stirred the food in the pan in front of her, watching the steam rise. Saying goodbye to her father was going to be hard, but their life had been a permanent pause for the last few weeks. She needed this. She needed closure. She needed to put an end to this chapter in her life so that maybe...maybe...the pain would be less. Maybe if it wasn't her *present*, then it wouldn't hurt every moment of every day just to breathe.

Maybe she'd be able to find happiness again. Maybe even with Grant.

CHAPTER ELEVEN

"I don't exercise," she groaned from down the hill behind him.

Grant turned around to look at a sweating, gasping Simone as she trekked up behind him in her tight spandex tank top and leggings. "Well, we *are* trying new things."

"Fun things! The speakeasy, the casino, windsurfing, the drive down Pacific Coast Highway? Those were fun. No one ever put 'more exercise' on their bucket list," she said, catching up to him and placing an arm on his shoulder to lean against him.

He grinned at her, loving the way her cheeks were bright red from exertion. They'd been going out a lot over the last week, and certainly knocked quite a few things off their combined bucket list, but he was clearly the more outdoorsy type out of the two of them. He didn't mind one bit, though. Her theatrics were part of the reason he loved spending so much time with her. She could always make him laugh, and even doing the most mundane things, like working together, was always fun when Simone was there.

Simone let out a long exhale. "I hate you. How are you not even sweating yet?"

He laughed, glancing down at his chest. True to form, his shirt was completely dry. He worked out pretty often, so it took a lot more than a small climb up the side of a hill to make him feel the burn. He offered her his water bottle. "Do you want some water?"

"God, yes." She took it and quickly drank at least half of it. "Ah. Much better."

"Ready for the last half to the top?"

Simone's eyes widened. "We're *only* halfway there?"

Grant took her hand, laughing. "Come on, you baby. It's not that far. It'll be worth it."

"It's a giant sign, Grant. One we can't even legally go near, so..."

"The Hollywood sign is a staple of living here. You can't be a Los Angeles native and never have gone to see it in person."

Simone shrugged. "I see it in person all the time."

"That doesn't count when it's from a distance." Grant squeezed her hand. "It'll be worth it. I promise."

"Okay, but let it go on record that I'm being held hostage against my will and forced to perform torturous activities. You could be arrested, you know."

Grant laughed again, leaning over and kissing her cheek. "You're absolutely ridiculous, you know that?"

"Maybe," she teased, clearly calming down now as they slowed their walk.

Her hand was warm in his, but he liked it. He liked everything about having her next to him. She'd shared his bed the majority of the nights since they'd met, and they spent all their free time together but it never felt like enough. He found himself thinking about her all the time and counting down the moment until they next saw each other again.

"You know, I've been to jail," she suddenly said.

Grant glanced at her through his peripheral. "Uh...what?"

She nodded. "Yep. In high school, I spent the night in jail when I was caught drinking at a house party. Everyone else's parents came and picked them up, but mine made me spend the night to 'teach me a lesson.'" She made air quotes around the last part. "It was really rude."

"Sounds like you deserved it," he teased, not wanting to think about his own impending jail time. Fingers crossed he would be able to avoid it.

"Maybe," she said with a small laugh. "Either way, I didn't talk to my parents for two weeks. My dad was such a hard-ass back then. What about you?"

He shrugged. "What about me?"

"Ever been in trouble with the law? Am I dating a bad boy?"

Grant chuckled, but nerves scattered through his stomach. "Uh, I'm no stranger to the legal system."

She waited a beat, giving him a chance to explain. He wasn't about to lie to her, but there was no fucking way he was going to tell her that there was a warrant out for his arrest and he had a list of white collar crimes against him.

"Feel free to be less mysterious," she teased. "I told you mine!"

He pulled her closer to his side as they walked. "Is this tit for tat now?"

"It's only fair—" Her shoe suddenly caught on a rock and she stumbled.

Grant reached out quickly and caught her right before she hit the ground. "Are you okay?"

"Whoa." She took a deep breath. "Yeah, I'm fine. Thanks for the assist."

"We're almost to the top. Come on, let's double time it, and we'll be there in minutes." He squeezed her hand tighter in his, guiding them up the hill at a faster pace.

She moved quickly to keep up with him, but she didn't look fooled for one moment. He had no doubt she could tell that he was avoiding answering the question, but he hoped if they were out of breath, she couldn't ask again. Sure enough, within a minute, she was huffing and puffing beside him and conversation was impossible.

"I fucking hate this," she gasped between breaths. "This sign better be worth it."

A few minutes later, they reached the top of the hill, and stared down at the back of the Hollywood sign below them.

"Wow," Simone said. "DoowylloH. Certainly never seen the sign backwards before. It is beautiful though."

Grant laughed. "Look at this view." He gestured toward the valley below them.

Sure enough, Los Angeles and the surrounding area stretched out beneath them like a blanket of hills and valleys covered in patches of thick urban developments and strolling dessert suburbs. The Hollywood sign itself was surrounded by fencing with signs to stay out, but it was still strikingly beautiful to see such a giant structure so close. The massive strength of each letter shadowing across the city below was stunning, and it was one of his favorite spots in all of America.

"Let's set up here." He pointed to a flat area not too far away. They walked over and he took off his backpack, opening it up to pull out a blanket. With a quick shake, he laid it flat across the dirt and then pulled out the bottle of wine and box of crackers they'd brought with them.

Simone stretched out across the blanket, lying flat on her back and looking up at the sun. "This is my favorite part of the hike so far."

"Lying down?"

"And wine," she added, sitting up and pulling two paper cups out of his backpack. "Never forget the wine."

He opened it quickly—thanks to the ease of a screw-top—and poured them both some.

"We need to toast," she said, taking the glass from him and sniffing the wine.

"What are we toasting to this time?" he asked, seated himself next to her.

"The way you make me feel," she replied, lifting her glass to his. "Here's to butterflies."

He tapped his glass against hers. "I give you butterflies?"

She nodded her head, a slight blush creeping up her already-red cheeks. "Is that bad to say? Too soon? It's only been a few weeks."

"It's never too soon for honesty." He kissed her neck, breathing in the scent of her shampoo. "It feels like time stand stills with us. Do you know what I mean? Like we've been here forever...been together forever."

She nuzzled her nose against his cheek as she turned her head to face him. "I know what you mean."

"You're not the only one with butterflies," he finally said after a long moment of silence.

He could feel her smile against his cheek where her head was leaning.

"I know," she replied.

"How are you feeling about tomorrow?" he asked after a few moments of silence.

Simone sighed, shaking her head lightly. "I'm not looking forward to it...and I am. The memorial is going to be huge. A ridiculous amount of people RSVP'd. It should be a beautiful event, and I know my mother really needs it."

"I'm honored you asked me to go with you," he admitted. "But I'm also a little nervous. I don't know what to do or say to make you feel better. I've never lost a parent. I've suffered loss, but I can't pretend to know what you're going through. I'm just so sorry. Is there anything I can do?"

"There's nothing I need you to do." She leaned up and kissed his cheek. "But you're sweet to worry. Just having you there. Just knowing you'll be by my side...that's more than enough."

He didn't reply, but it honestly didn't feel like enough. At the same time, part of him was nervous about how serious everything felt. It was insanely selfish to even think that way—he knew that and hated himself for it—but at the same time, he couldn't stop the slight panic in his gut at the idea of going to such a serious family event as her date. They'd agreed to date for one month—just for fun. It wasn't supposed to be serious. It wasn't supposed to be *real.*

This felt really fucking real. And he didn't hate it. That was the weirdest part. He *wanted* to be there for her. He wanted to help her through this and have her lean on him.

He wanted to be her person, and that scared the shit out of him.

CHAPTER TWELVE

"That was a beautiful ceremony," Aria said, wiping a tissue under her eyes. "Dad would have really loved how many people came."

The entire Reynolds family was standing in the church's vestibule, having just said goodbye to each and every one of the over one hundred guests who'd attended their father's memorial. Ben had his arms around Aria, and Reed had cut his trip short to be able to be here for Teagan. She leaned into his side, her hand on her stomach. Her pregnancy was still a secret, but Simone warmed at knowing that their father knew his future grandbaby had been there.

Everything about today had gone perfectly. People had shared stories and memories, and the minister had given a short sermon about grief and love. The church had been beautifully decorated, and everyone who'd been there had commented on what a wonderful time they'd had. Despite the sad purpose for being there, everyone had been in a great mood. The stories had brought laughter and happiness, and they'd reveled in the joy of remembering who Jack

Reynolds had been and how much of an impact he'd had on every one of their lives.

Simone nodded. "It was a great day."

The front door opened and Grant walked in. He held up a set of car keys and then handed them to her. "Pulled the car up front so you don't have to walk all the way back to the lot," he said.

She'd been the one to drive her mother there and the lot had been so full of cars that she'd had to park a ridiculous distance away. Simone put her hand over her chest. "That was really sweet, Grant."

He shrugged, kissing her temple and wrapping an arm around her waist. "It's been a long day. I figured you were probably tired."

That was definitely true. The sheer emotional journey of today had exhausted her, and she felt like she could go to bed right now and not wake up until tomorrow.

"Thank you, Grant," Betty spoke up, placing her hand on his forearm. "That was very gentlemanly of you. I'm glad my Simmy has found such a great man."

Simone could feel the heat rising in her cheeks. "Mom..."

"What?" Betty replied, shrugging her shoulders. "I think your father would definitely have approved, too." Tears rimmed her eyes, and Aria handed her a tissue which she quickly used to wipe her eyes. "It's been a great day, girls. All of you—" She gestured toward the entire family. "All of you have made today beautiful for Jack. I know he's looking down on all of us and smiling right now. Thank you. Thank you for making today as easy for me as you could."

Simone stepped forward and wrapped her arms around her mother. "We love you, Mom."

Aria and Teagan joined, and it turned into a group hug for a moment until they all finally let go.

"All right. Enough crying," their mother said, taking a deep breath. "Let's go on home and have dinner. I'm starving."

"That sounds like a good idea," Aria replied. "The food should be ready by now."

Aria had had her private chef cook dinner at their mother's house for the entire family so it would be ready by the time the memorial was over. Simone had done a lot of legwork for today's event, but her sisters had been with her every step of the way. She couldn't thank them enough for everything they'd done to help. Honestly, it was amazing to see the entire family come together like they had today. They'd always been close, but this was different. This was even more than she'd ever expected, and she knew her father would be happy to see them all coming together like this.

Grant was standing to the side, talking with Ben and Reed. She couldn't help but smile to see him being a part of this. He was laughing with her brothers-in-law and, honestly, he fit in seamlessly. They'd only been dating a short time now, but he looked like he belonged. Her family already loved him and she...well, she wasn't going to say that she loved him. That wasn't an option. It was off the table. He was leaving at the end of the month, and then...nothing. That was it.

She swallowed hard, her heart squeezing at the thought. She'd promised herself that she'd be okay with their arrangement. And she was...or at least, she had been. But every morning that she woke up next to him, every night that she fell asleep in his arms...it seemed harder and harder to think about the day coming where he wouldn't be there anymore.

"Ready to go?" Grant asked, suddenly standing right in front of her.

She blinked, pushing away the distracting thoughts of their imminent ending. "Yeah. Are you coming back to the house with us for dinner?"

He shook his head. "I think I'm going to let you all enjoy some family time together. I don't want to intrude."

"You wouldn't be intruding," she assured him. "You've been amazing all day."

"Well, you needed me here." He pulled her into his embrace, kissing her gently. "I'll always be there if you need me, Simone."

"At least for a few more weeks." She swallowed hard at the thought, knowing she probably shouldn't have even said that, but somehow unable to stop herself.

Grant frowned. "No. Forever. I'm only ever a phone call away."

Part of her didn't even want to hear that. She didn't want that hope, that lingering *maybe*. But the other part of her warmed at the reminder that even though they had a deadline, they were always going to be a part of each other's lives. Being together had impacted both of them, and that would never go away.

Even when they were apart.

"Thank you," she finally said, kissing him back. "I really appreciate that."

He lowered his voice, leaning toward her ear. "Call me later tonight, okay? After dinner. If you want some company."

She smiled, her tongue sliding across her lower lip. "Are you asking me to booty call you, Mr. Mercer?"

He chuckled lightly, rubbing his hands up and down her arms. "My booty is yours to call anytime, Ms. Reynolds."

She couldn't hide her grin, laughing at the very imagery. Only Grant could bring humor to such a heavy moment. She loved the way he knew when she needed that relief.

"I'll see you tonight then," she replied. Leaning up on the tips of her toes, she kissed him one more time and then watched him leave. Turning, she wound her way back around the vestibule to find her mother. "Mom? You ready to go?"

Betty stood at the front of the church in front of a large photograph of Jack. She let out a loud sigh. "I'm ready. I guess I have to be."

"We can stay longer," Simone assured her, but her mother shook her head.

"No. I'm ready." She squeezed Simone's hands, then linked their arms together and walked back down the aisle. "Let's go. It's time."

Simone felt a frown pulling at the corners of her lips. "Are you okay, Mom?"

Her mother nodded slowly, keeping her gaze forward. "I will be."

That was exactly how she felt, too. She wasn't okay with losing her father. She wasn't okay with losing Grant in only a few weeks. Maybe less. But she would be.

She had to be.

CHAPTER THIRTEEN

"I can't believe you've lived here your whole life and never gone surfing," Grant said, shaking his head. "I only come here a few times a year, and even I get out on the water more than that."

"Well, I still go swimming and boating and all that. That counts as out on the water." Simone shrugged her shoulders. "I just never learned how to surf. It looks pretty complicated."

Grant lifted the rented surfboard from the sandy beach and leaned against it. "Well, today's the day."

She grinned, picking up her rental surfboard as well. "You better be my lifeguard, too. I'm not about to get swept out to sea in a wave."

She didn't need to worry about that. Grant stepped closer to her, lowering his voice. "I'd never let anything happen to you."

A visible shiver rippled through her, the sight sending a similar thrill through him. They'd already spent all morning in his bed, but he was more than ready to go again anytime he looked at her. Every moment they weren't in the studio rehearsing, they were either in bed or working on another item on her bucket list. Honestly, it was the busiest, yet most fun, month of his entire life. They were making every second count.

"Promises, promises," she replied, a tiny smile on one half of her lips. "Come on. Let's get wet."

He growled slightly. "I better get in that water before I create a scene on this beach." His eyes flickered down to his crotch where he was already becoming hard.

Simone giggled and lifted her surfboard above her head, racing to the water's edge. "First one in wins!"

Grant took off after her, reaching the water at the same time as she did and paddling in deeper. "Beat you!"

"That was a tie!" she insisted, smacking his shoulder with a splash of sea water. She shimmied on to the top of her surfboard, laying across it and using her arms to guide her farther into the sea.

Grant joined her closer to where the waves were breaking and then spent a good five minutes explaining to her how to hop up on her board and catch a wave inbound for the shore. After a few practice runs, she had the general concept down, but not the actual skill to implement it just yet. Wave after wave, she plummeted into the sea and slid off the surfboard, but each time she came up, she was laughing.

It was one of the things he absolutely loved about her. Or...uh...liked about her. Not love. This definitely wasn't love. Grant swallowed hard at the very thought of that word. Spending the last week with her family and the preparations for her father's funeral had been an incredibly intimate time together that felt like it had sped up the dating process. They'd somehow gone from casual and just sleeping together to suddenly being involved in the most painful moments of her life. Their relationship had grown and normally, that would be a good thing.

But not now. Not for him.

He was only two short weeks away from going to London to work on his next project. There was no telling when he'd be back in Los Angeles, except maybe the short time around the movie's live stream and marketing push. That made a relationship impossible between them already, not to mention the fact that his own personal life was so complicated. He wouldn't subject Simone to any of that.

An hour later, the duo climbed out of the ocean and collapsed on the hot sand a good distance from the water's edge.

"That was incredible," Simone panted, still catching her breath.

"You literally fell off the board every single time," Grant pointed out.

She didn't seem to care one bit. "I stayed up at least five seconds on that last one!"

Grant laughed, staring up at the clouds above them. "Fair."

Simone turned on to her side and propped her head up on her hand. "We've been doing so many new things over the last couple of weeks. I feel like my bucket list is almost complete."

"What's left on there?"

She shrugged and lay back on the sand. "Nothing."

Grant sat up, furrowing his brows. There was something she wasn't saying. "There's got to be something else."

"Well, there is...but it's not really anything I can cross off."

"Tell me," he prodded, scooping a handful of sand in his palm and gently pouring it across her leg.

She watched him intently. "You're going to think it sounds stupid. Or cliché."

"So?" Grant shrugged. "It doesn't matter what anyone thinks but you."

Simone nodded her head slowly. "The only thing I've ever really wanted to cross off my bucket list is to fall in love. The last time I got close, he was only using me for my connections. Other than that, I've never dated anyone seriously."

Grant felt a pang of guilt that he was adding to that. They certainly weren't serious, and never going to be, despite the lingering wish in the back of his mind that that could change. "You've *never* been in love? Not even childhood love?"

She shook her head. "Nope. What about you? You've been in love, right? I mean, you were married."

"I was married. I thought we were in love." He stopped, not really wanting to say more than that. "But you may have a point."

"Well, what happened?"

Grant glanced up at her, then just shook his head. "It didn't work out."

Simone tossed a handful of sand at his chest. "Come on, Grant. You never open up about your life. You never tell me anything."

"I don't like to think about it, Simone," he replied, but he knew that she wasn't going to be satisfied with that answer. "Yes, I was in love with my ex-wife. Or a type of love. What I thought was love at the time, but now that I look back on it...maybe I never really knew what love was at all. Maybe I'm just like you." He sighed deeply. "She ran off with my best friend and broke my fucking heart, leaving me a huge mess to deal with that I'm still cleaning up. Is that what you want to hear? That my entire life is in shambles and I can't even remember the last time I felt whole?"

His voice was racketing louder and grittier with every word, and when he finally came to a stop, he realized that he was close to tears. Clearing his throat, he tried to push away the emotions he wasn't ready to feel. Honestly, it wasn't even entirely true. Being around Simone? It was the most whole and happy he'd felt since his marriage had been happy. She was a bright light in his dark life, and he wanted to tell her that, but he was sure if he kept talking, he was going to cry.

And he didn't fucking cry.

Simone was quiet for a moment, then leaned in and took his hand. "I'm sorry, Grant. I'm so sorry you had to go through that."

He squeezed her hand back, nodding instead of responding.

"Stories like that make me think it's better that I've never been in love," she continued. "Maybe it's not worth the heart break."

Grant shook his head, because despite everything he'd been through, he wouldn't go back and change a thing. "That's not true. Not at all. Being in love...it's invigorating. It's fulfilling. It's the answer to every question you didn't know you were asking. Even when it ends...even when it hurts...it's worth it to have felt it once. Even if what I felt was only a fraction of the real thing."

Simone's jaw tensed. Her voice lowered, almost to a whisper. Tentative and nervous. "Do you think...do you think we would have fallen in love? If you weren't leaving?"

Grant took a second before he answered, nibbling on the corner of his bottom lip. He wanted to say yes. He wanted to say part of him already had. But that wasn't an option, and he wasn't going to leave her with hope when there was none. That just seemed cruel. "I don't think I could fall in love with anyone right now. My life is...it's complicated."

The crestfallen look on her face was evident, but she quickly masked it with a small, tight-lipped smile and nod. "Life is complicated. I think that's how it's supposed to be for everyone. I'm certainly no stranger to it."

"True, but I...there are things you don't know about me yet. Things I can't subject anyone to." Like the warrant out for his arrest or the possible jail time he was facing when he returned home.

"I want to, though," she replied, her voice still soft and her fingers caressing his forearm. "I want to know everything about you."

There was pain in her words now, and he began to wonder if this was a mistake. If the last few weeks were meaning too much to her, and that he was only going to hurt her when he left. That was the last thing he wanted, and yet...fuck, it *was* going to hurt. It was going to hurt like hell to say goodbye to her.

But the last thing he wanted was for her to feel that, too.

"Simone..." He paused, letting out a deep breath. "We agreed."

"I know, I know," she said, a heaviness to her words. "Casual. I know."

They stared quietly out at the ocean in front of them, the waves licking the shore every few seconds. He wanted to pull her against him, kiss her until she forgot everything, but instead, they just stayed like that. Side by side. Angry at the upcoming goodbye and hurting at the inability to change a thing.

This was what they'd signed up for. He couldn't change his mind now.

CHAPTER FOURTEEN

"So TAUNT me and hurt me, deceive me, desert me..." Simone took a deep breath between lyrics from the musical, leaning against the side of the piano in his hotel living room. "I'm yours 'til I die, so in love, so in love, so in love with you, my love, am I."

Grant played the final chords in the song before lifting his hands from the piano keys. "That was perfect, Simone."

It had been three weeks since they'd met and started practicing together, and she was more than ready for filming to start. They'd continue to practice for another week, but he had no doubt that she was going to knock her performance out of the park.

"Thank you," she replied. "I've been working my voice a lot lately. I have a performance this weekend in Las Vegas."

Their tension on the beach a few days ago had been forgotten. Or, more likely, buried. They both knew their time was coming to a close, but neither wanted to acknowledge it or bring it up again. He certainly didn't. They'd fallen back into their previous patterns—work, sex, dates. It was just as wonderful as before, even with the looming deadline of their eventual parting in only a week.

Grant lifted one brow. "Vegas? Ever been before?"

She shook her head. "No, but I'm opening for the *American Voice* winner for the entire weekend. They're headlining a month long show there."

"That's a big deal." Grant had already been super impressed with how far she'd gotten on the reality singing competition, but to turn that into continued work afterwards was something few people could do unless they really hustled. The competition had only ended a little over a month ago and she'd already championed it into more success afterwards. From what he could tell, Simone was never not working—whether on her singing or for her family. "When do you leave?"

"Tonight. I was thinking..." She paused for a moment, her fingers fidgeting. "What if you came with me? Another first to explore..."

He briefly considered her proposal, but there was zero chance that he was going to say no. "That sounds fun. Sin City...sure you're ready for that? I've been a few times and it can get pretty wild."

"Oh, I'm ready," she replied. "You just try to keep up."

Grant laughed, loving her confidence. He'd loved every minute of getting to know her and was already beginning to dread leaving. It was depressing the hell out of him.

Simone slid into his lap, circling her arms around his neck. "Is traveling together too much too soon?"

He shook his head. "I don't think there's a list of rules to follow for our kind of dating."

"The kind with an expiration date," she replied.

He wasn't entirely sure, but he could have sworn a look

of disappointment crossed her face. Was she dreading the end of their month together, too?

"Exactly," Grant continued. "We make up our own rules."

She nuzzled his cheek with her nose, brushing her lips against his jaw. "You don't follow any rules."

Grant chuckled. That was definitely true. "I like my freedom." Ironic, since he might be losing that the moment he touched down in New Zealand. But honestly, freedom wasn't as appealing as it once had been, knowing he was leaving her behind.

Reaching around her, he pulled the cover closed over the piano keys, then gripped Simone's waist and lifted her to sit on top of the piano.

"Hey!" She squeaked at the sudden transition.

He grinned, pushing apart her knees and settling on the bench in between them. Softly, he kissed the inside of her knees. With gentle strokes of his lips and tongue, he moved up her inner thigh.

Her eyes immediately hooded as she watched him, her hands gripping the hem of her skirt and sliding it up farther for him.

Grant chuckled. "Someone's eager."

Simone leaned back on her elbows, watching him. "Mmm."

When he reached her core, he discovered that she wasn't wearing any panties. He lifted one brow and looked up at her. "Going bare?"

"Only when I'm with you," she teased, her tongue sliding across her bottom lip.

He liked that answer. Growling low in his chest, he pushed her legs wider apart, setting her feet on his knees to support her. His mouth found her core quickly, long slow licks across her center that had her moaning and thrusting her hips against him.

With tauntingly slow circles, he wrapped his tongue around her clit, knowing waves of near orgasms were already spiraling through her at the very feel. He lifted his hand and slid one finger inside her, groaning at how warm and wet she felt against his skin. She squeezed him, and he wasn't sure he could wait much longer to have his dick inside her.

She gasped, her body shaking as her first orgasm hit her hard. He didn't stop licking or thrusting his finger in and out until her body finally slowed and melted against the piano.

"Holy shit..." She groaned.

Unzipping his pants, Grant fisted his dick as he sat on the piano bench beneath her. Reaching into his pocket, he pulled out a condom and made quick work of putting it on. "You're so fucking hot when you come, Simone."

She pushed up on her elbows, eyeing him. Her tongue slid across her lower lip. "I need you."

Grant grabbed her by her waist and pulled her down from on top of the piano so that she was straddling his waist. They wasted no time as she grabbed his dick and positioned him at her entrance. With one long push, she slid down his shaft, taking every inch of him.

"Oh, God..." Moans parted her lips before he kissed her.

Their mouths danced together as she bounced up and down on top of him, their chests pressed tightly together as their arms circled one another. It was like he couldn't get close enough no matter how on top of each other they were. Every part of her body called to his, like a siren he couldn't help but answer to.

Knowing that in less than a week they'd be parted...hell, it killed him.

He'd dated plenty before getting married, but nothing that ever lasted more than one or two dinners. Somehow, he'd spent almost every other day with Simone—sometimes every day. When they weren't working or she wasn't with her family, she was in his bed and he loved every second of it. They went to dinners, took long hikes that she hated, went swimming at the beach, and had made it their mission to constantly try new things together.

It had been a whirlwind adventure that was supposed to be no pressure. Somehow, though, their impending deadline seemed to only up the ante. It was like he wanted to squeeze in as much as he could before he left for London, but at the same time, he wanted to leave now and avoid the entire heartbreak of goodbye.

Heartbreak? Grant tried to push the idea out of his mind.

They were just dating. Casually. This wasn't love. His heart wasn't invested.

"I'm close," Simone said, pulling him back into the moment as their bodies slid together in harmony.

"Come on me," he instructed, a slight growl following his words as his fingers dug into her hips, guiding her up and down on his cock.

He was only seconds behind when she finally unraveled. Her head fell forward, resting against his shoulder as her body shook against him. His own climax pulsed through him, sending warm waves of pleasure through every nerve. She slowed, sitting quietly on top of him as they both waited for the excitement to subside.

"That was amazing." She scattered soft kisses against his neck. "Absolutely amazing."

"You're not so bad yourself," he teased, finding her lips with his.

They kissed softly, gently, until finally he lifted her from him and went to go clean up. His phone buzzed in his pocket as he was turning off the faucet. He dried his hands on a towel and then pulled it out, reading the new email notification on the screen.

"Fuck." He shook his head, shoving the phone back in his pocket.

He exited the bathroom and found Simone standing by the window, looking out on Los Angeles below. "Simone?"

"Hmm?" She turned to face him, her lips swollen and her cheeks blush red.

He took her in his arms, kissing her cheek and then her lips. "They want me early in London. I've got to be there in the morning."

Her eyes widened and she stepped back. "What?"

"I can't make it to Las Vegas," he continued. "They moved up the shooting schedule for the London project. I've got to be there in time to work with the director on finishing the music."

Simone shook her head, hugging herself as she wrapped her arms around her waist. "Shit."

"I know." He hated the look of disappointment on her face.

"I thought we had more time," she continued. "But... you're leaving. And you're not coming back."

"I wouldn't say that," he objected, stepping closer to her again. She shrugged out of his arms and walked over to the couch. "I still come to Los Angeles once a year. Sometimes more."

"A year is a long time from now. Who knows where I'll be then?"

Grant pushed his hands into his pockets. "We knew this

was coming, Simone. This was always going to end. I don't know what to tell you...we knew."

"That's all you have to say? *We knew?*" Simone's brows furrowed. "I know we knew. It's been the dark cloud hanging over our head since day one. Why did we even do this then, if that's all you have to say?"

Grant blinked, trying to think of what to say. He wasn't minimizing their time together, but at the same time, there was nothing he could do about their lives being so different. They were heading in opposite directions, and as much as a big part of him wished they weren't...they were.

Fuck, he really wished things were different.

"I've really enjoyed our time together," he began, reaching for one of her hands. She reluctantly let him hold it but kept space between them. "I'm going to miss you. I'm going to miss what we've had."

He wanted to tell her how much he cared about her. How his heart was growing to maybe even—no. He couldn't say any of that. He couldn't tell her what he was really feeling when he was leaving. That would just hurt her for no reason.

"I'm going to miss us, too," she replied, stepping in to his embrace and wrapping her arms around his neck. "I don't know how to say goodbye. I wasn't ready for it to be today."

He held her tighter, breathing in the scent of her shampoo as her hair tickled his cheek. "I wasn't ready yet, either."

She pulled away just enough to look at his face. "I...I like you a lot, Grant."

He swallowed the lump in his throat, knowing she was saying so much more. "I like you, too, Simone."

"I have to go pack for Vegas. My flight is in a few hours."

He nodded, letting go of her.

She grabbed her purse on the table by the door and then turned around to face him. "Have fun in London."

"Have fun in Vegas," he replied.

They stared at each other awkwardly for a moment, as if neither one of them knew what to do or how to handle the moment. He wanted to run to her and kiss her, pull her back into his bed and make her miss her flight entirely.

But that wasn't life. That wasn't what they agreed to.

They'd agreed to temporary, and now temporary had ended.

CHAPTER FIFTEEN

"We only have two months left until we do this live," the director called out. "You all need to really step up your game because that was terrible."

"What?" Simone balked, stepping off the stage and making her way over to the cameras. "We were all pretty on point."

"Sure. You were all good," he replied. "But you weren't great. This is going to be *live*. There's no time for edits. No time for redos. Millions of people will be watching the broadcast from their living rooms and judging every single move we make. It has to be perfect."

He wasn't wrong. She knew that they were close, but they weren't there yet. Despite all of the practice, this was still a tough play and even tougher song and dance numbers. The entire crew had yet to come together as a cohesive unit, but she knew that the moment that happened, it would be perfection.

"Want to grab a drink?" Clara, one of the other actresses on the show, wrapped an arm around her shoulder, walking them over to the craft services table. "After practice tonight? I could certainly use some time to unwind."

Simone nodded, grabbing a bottle of water and taking a long swig. "That sounds fun. I need to get out more often. I've been a hermit ever since..."

She trailed off, not wanting to finish that sentence. She wasn't about to admit to her coworkers that she'd been sleeping with their musical director for almost a month until he up and left for another country. Hell, she knew better than to tarnish her reputation. They'd been careful to keep their romance away from work, so even though her family knew, and a few close friends, no one from set had figured out their involvement.

"Since what?" Clara pried.

"Nothing." Simone shrugged. "I've just had a bit of a dry spell lately."

"Ooh!" Clara clapped her hands together. "We can go out and pick up guys. I'm a great wing woman."

Simone shook her head. "I don't think I'm ready to date right now."

"Who said anything about dating?" Clara teased. "I'm just talking about for tonight."

Simone laughed, but there was no way. She wasn't a hook-up type of girl, despite the way her romance with Grant had started. It just wasn't in her blood. She needed commitment and feelings, and all of hers were still tangled up in Grant. "Maybe soon, but not today."

Despite not being ready today, she wasn't going to stay celibate forever. She knew she needed to move on from Grant eventually, but he'd only just left a few days ago. Hell, she could still smell his shampoo on her pillow cases. She definitely needed more time.

Her phone buzzed in her pocket. Pulling it out, she read Grant's name.

Good night, beautiful.

The time difference between them put them on opposite schedules, but he had yet to miss a single night where he wished her goodnight, or a single morning where he wished her good morning. It was sweet and made her feel all warm and fuzzy, but as much as that made her smile, she also hated it.

It was impossible to move on when he was gone...and yet, wasn't.

Good night, Grant. She sent a quick text back, and then added a kissing emoji. She needed to stop and just not respond, but...today wasn't that day.

"Let's get back on set. We're going back to the start of the second act," the director called out.

Simone quickly finished her bottle of water and then tossed it in the trash. Today was going to be a long day, but, still, she loved every moment of it.

As hard as the last few weeks had been with her father's memorial and Grant leaving, her work had been the one thing to keep her grounded. Going on stage and being someone entirely different was exactly what she needed. Every one of her problems disappeared for those few minutes, and she was only there to dazzle the audience. She was only there to tell someone else's story.

She'd been worried when she first took this role that acting wouldn't be for her. She was a singer—and that's where her passion always would lie. But at the same time, she'd fallen in love with the freedom of stepping into someone else's shoes, even if only for a little while.

Simone would go home tonight and sleep alone. She

would miss Grant and wonder what she was doing with her life. But Lilli, the lead in *Kiss Me, Kate*? She'd be on stage and damn happy driving Fred crazy.

And for a few hours, everything would be okay.

CHAPTER SIXTEEN

"I DON'T HAVE time for dating," Simone told Teagan, leaning against the bar they were both seated at.

Teagan took another sip of her soda, her hand smoothing across her pregnant belly. "I didn't say you had to make a full-time job out of it. Just get back out there. It's been over a month since Grant left and you're still padding around the house in your pajamas most weekend nights."

"I'm out right now," Simone argued, pointing around them to the bar full of people in downtown Los Angeles.

She still couldn't believe she'd let her sister talk her into going out, but she had to admit that Teagan did have a point. She spent her entire week practicing and prepping for the live-streamed movie premiere of *Kiss Me, Kate* that was only two weeks away. The entire cast would be performing the play live on camera while it played for millions of viewers at the same time. Any mistake would be noticed, so practice had been sixteen-hour days for the last month...and would be until the day of shooting.

"Barely. I've seen you check your phone every few minutes since we sat down."

Simone shrugged. "Well...we still text here and there."

"I don't understand you two's relationship," Teagan said with a loud sigh. "Are you together? Long-distance?"

"We're definitely not together," Simone clarified, though admittedly, she wished they were. She felt so dumb even thinking that, but she lived for those few moments a day when a text message from Grant lit up her phone. Sure, they kept things PG, and he never pushed for more, but the friendship they'd developed still mattered just as much to her.

She wished she'd told him in his hotel room exactly how much their month together—well, more like three-and-a-half-weeks—had meant to her. She wished she'd told him how strong her feelings were, how much she'd really miss him...but that would have been ridiculous.

No one fell in love after three weeks.

She could feel her cheeks heating at the very idea. She was *not* in love. Definitely not. No way. Couldn't happen. Maybe her sister was right. She needed a new perspective, a new adventure. She needed to move on from the man she was never going to see again. He'd made very clear that they had been temporary. They were over.

"Miss?" The bartender came over and placed a glass in front of her. "The gentleman at the end of the bar sent this over for you. Amaretto sour."

"Simone!" Teagan grabbed her forearm. "If this isn't a sign, I don't know what is."

Simone glanced down at the rocks glass in front of her. She never would have ordered that drink, but...it was still a sweet gesture.

"Go over and thank him," Teagan encouraged, pushing the drink toward her. "This could be exactly what you need."

She chewed on the bottom of her lip, trying to decide. "Really? You don't think it's a little weird to send a drink over that only a sixteen-year-old would like?"

Teagan shrugged. "At least he made an effort. Does Grant make any effort? No. He's off living his life on another continent."

Simone rolled her eyes. "Okay. Okay. Point taken." She leaned over the bar, glancing down toward the end. *Holy shit.* The man sitting in the last bar seat was hot as hell. Jet black hair slicked back, he had a late-night stubble across his chin and two arms completely covered with tattoos. Everything about him screamed 'bad boy,' and, admittedly, that had always been a weakness of hers. Hell, Grant was probably the only man she'd ever dated that hadn't been full of ink and bad attitudes. Though his long hair and foreign accent could make a case for him.

"Shit, he's cute." Simone picked up the glass he'd sent over. "Okay, wish me luck."

"Good luck!" Teagan said. "Oh, and don't take too long. I don't want to be sitting here forever alone and pregnant."

"I'm just going to say thank you, then I'll be right back," Simone assured her. She certainly had no plans on ditching her sister for a guy.

Walking across the bar, she made her way to the man at the end. "Excuse me?"

He turned around on his stool, a glass of dark liquor in his hand. "I was hoping you'd come over and say hi," he replied, a slightly crooked smile on his face. "I didn't want to interrupt you with your friend there."

Simone smiled. "My sister, actually. I just wanted to thank you for the drink. It was very sweet."

"I hope it's a kind you like." He tipped his glass to hers,

clinking them together. "I wasn't sure what a pretty girl like yourself would be drinking."

She laughed lightly, taking a sip from the glass. It was very sugary, but not terrible. "I actually haven't had one of these since I was using a fake ID to sneak into clubs."

The man grinned. "Swing and a miss then. I'm Jax, by the way."

"Jack?" Simone's eyes widened. That was her father's name, and though he'd been gone a few months, it still felt like yesterday.

"J-A-X." His lopsided grin warmed her chest. "Not Jack."

"Oh, I like that spelling," she admitted. "It's a little eclectic. Not sure I've met anyone named Jax before."

"Glad to be your first," he replied, winking at her this time. He patted the open stool next to him. "Care to sit and have a drink with me?"

She gestured back toward Teagan. "I actually have to get back to my sister, but...thank you."

"Ah, okay." Jax nodded his head. "Can I at least get your number before you go...uh, I don't think I got your name?"

Simone hesitated for a moment, glancing back toward Teagan who was gesturing for her to go for it. "Simone, and, um...I guess so. Why not?"

"Exactly. Why not?" He pulled out his phone from his pocket and the two traded numbers.

"It was good to meet you, Jax." She let a small smile steal over her lips.

"Even better to meet you, Simone," he replied.

She quickly scurried back to Teagan, sliding back onto the bar stool she'd left open. "Oh. My. God."

"Well? How was it?" her sister asked.

"He's really hot," Simone admitted. "We exchanged phone numbers."

Teagan pumped her hands in the air. "Yes! Finally. You know the best way to get over a man?"

"Get under another one?" Simone laughed and shook her head. "I have no plans on sleeping with anyone anytime soon. Grant was...well, he's going to be hard to forget in that department."

"All the more reason to get back out there and try." Teagan took another sip of her soda. "Come on. We should probably head back to the house. See how Mom's doing."

"She did some gardening today," Simone said. "It was pretty amazing to see. I haven't seen her in the garden since before Dad died. Maybe longer."

"Slowly but surely, she's coming out of her shell," Teagan agreed. "But with the six-month anniversary coming up soon...I'm worried she might backslide."

"I think that's normal though, right? I mean, to backslide on anniversaries?"

Teagan nodded. "Probably. Still...I can't even imagine what she must be feeling."

"She's got us." Simone downed the last of her glass. "And don't worry, I'm not going anywhere."

"Are you sure about that? I might have heard a rumor..." Teagan lifted one brow, staring pointedly at her.

"What rumor?"

Teagan leaned her elbow against the bar. "I heard you might be coming to New York soon."

Simone felt her cheeks heating. She hadn't told anyone about the call she'd gotten last week. She was in the running for the lead role in the Broadway show of *Anastasia*, a story she'd loved since she was a little girl. Her agent had delivered the good news, but she hadn't told a soul. Why would she? It wasn't a certainty, and, to be honest, she was quite sure that she wouldn't get the role. The other players up for it were old names to the Broadway stage and blew her experience out of the water.

"It's been talked about," Simone admitted. "But it's a long shot. Like loooooong shot. Don't get your hopes up."

Teagan grinned and Simone could tell it was already too late. "You and I could be neighbors! It's about time I had someone on the East Coast with me. It's lonely back there."

"You've been in Los Angeles more than New York this year," Simone pointed out.

"True, but Reed's almost done promoting his upcoming movie. Then we'll both have three months off. We're going to travel with Piper before the baby is born. A little mini-babymoon."

"That sounds amazing," Simone said, sliding her credit card into the checkbook the bartender dropped off. "I definitely need to travel more. One of my friends just got back from a nudist spa resort outside of Palm Springs and was telling me all about it. That's the kind of crazy thing I should be doing right now."

"Probably not the best place for a babymoon, but you have fun," Teagan teased. "So...are you going to call him?"

"Who?"

Teagan scoffed. "The guy at the end of the bar. Obviously."

"Jax? Um...yeah? Probably." Simone chewed on the edge of her lip then thanked the bartender as he returned their check. "He seemed like a nice guy. I certainly am not attached to anyone right now."

"You're free as a bird," her sister agreed. "But you really should stop texting Grant."

Simone returned her credit card to her wallet. "We're just friends."

"People who have had sex can't just be friends. Penises make things complicated."

Her sister had a point. Talking to Grant wasn't as emotion-free as she tried to pretend it was. "I'll think about it. Maybe Jax will help distract me."

Maybe that was exactly what she needed.

CHAPTER SEVENTEEN

"Hello?" Simone knocked on the edge of a slightly ajar giant metal door, peeking her head inside. "Is anyone here?"

A tall figure stood over a work bench, a helmet over his face as sparks flew everywhere around him. A loud whirring filled the space, and as she drew closer, she realized he was shaping metal.

"Jax?" she called out again, louder this time.

The man paused and threw up his helmet, turning to face her. "Hey! Give me a second."

He quickly tossed his helmet and the thick apron he was wearing onto a nearby wooden table then walked over to a crusty looking sink in the corner and washed his hands. He wiped down his face and arms with a clean rag, then finally came over to her.

"I'm glad you came," he said, leaning in to give her a hug.

She returned his embrace, trying hard not to notice how good he smelled—a woodsy musk that screamed all man and made her stomach tighten with excitement. "Well, I was invited."

He laughed, a hardy laugh that she could feel vibrating

across her skin. "Well, of course you're invited. To be honest, though...you come across a little bit like a tiger with her tail caught. I'm worried if I let go you'll run away, or worse...I'll get the claws."

Simone couldn't stop herself from grinning. She liked the imagery, and she liked that she had him on his toes. "Better be careful then."

"Come on, let me show you around before we get started." He gestured for her to follow him.

"You still haven't told me what we're doing." She placed her purse down on a shelf against one wall. "Can I leave this here?"

"Let's put it in the cabinet," he advised, opening a small cabinet for her. She placed her purse inside and then he closed it behind them. "By the way, you look fantastic."

A blush crept up her cheeks. She was wearing tight, dark jeans under a thin white tank top, so she certainly hadn't dressed up, but he'd told her not to. There was no mistaking the way his eyes grazed her body, pausing on her breasts for a moment longer than she'd expected. She could feel her core heating up with every pass of his stare.

"Thank you," she replied. "Enough stalling. What's the big exciting idea you had?"

"We're racing." He reached out and laced his fingers through hers, then pulled her through the back door for the shop they were in. It exited out onto a small patch of grass separating them from a larger structure that looked a bit like an open garage. On the other side of the building, she could see the setup for a large race track.

"Racing?" Her eyes widened. Well, hell, she had said she was going to try new things.

"Ever been in a race car?" he asked, leading them to the

garage and then through to the track where several cars were parked on the track."

"Definitely not."

He glanced back at her, running his fingers up her arm this time. "Want to try?"

"Definitely," she said quickly, a grin already lighting up her face. "I mean, I'll probably wreck the car because I'm a terrible driver—"

"Nothing you can break that I can't fix," he assured her, leading them over to a green car on the edge of the track. "Climb on in the passenger side. I'll take us on a lap then let you do your own if you're ready."

"Okay!" Simone didn't need to be told twice. She quickly hopped into the passenger seat of the car and began buckling herself in.

Jax slid in next to her and turned the car on, also taking care to buckle himself in carefully. "Ready?"

Simone clutched the edge of her seat. "Yes!"

He slammed the car into drive and hit the gas so fast that she almost didn't feel them start. They were just suddenly flying in a flash of squealing tires and smoke and the track racing past her window.

"Ah!" She screamed as they rounded the first corner at the fastest speed she'd ever gone. It was exhilarating and exciting and everything she was craving in her life right now. The world whipped past her and she didn't miss it for a second. She was in her own little bubble, flying at break-neck speeds and leaving everything terrible behind her.

Jax knew exactly what he was doing. He was focused and concentrated, turning the car with precision and an execution that only years of practice could bring. When they were finally around the first bend and coming up on the second, she caught a glimpse of his face.

His jaw was set, tense, but the bright blues of his eyes were almost molten, filled with an excitement and passion she recognized in herself anytime she hit the stage. This track...this was his stage, and damn, he looked good performing on it.

Simone nibbled on the edge of her lip as they pulled back around to the starting line and he slowed to a stop. Oh, yeah, Jax was going to be one hell of a distraction.

"Well? What did you think?" he asked.

She could still feel her heart beating at the pace they'd been driving. "I think we should go again. And again. And again. Just to be sure, you know?"

He laughed, reached over, and squeezed her hand. "Anything you want, baby."

Admittedly, she liked that term of endearment even though this was only their first date. They'd texted a bit over the last two days, but she had always been more of the type to get to know someone in person rather than through her phone.

"You're really going to let me drive this?" she asked.

He shrugged. "Sure. Why not?"

She unbuckled her seatbelt and climbed out of the car while he did the same. "I could be a terrible driver. I could crash and kill us both."

"Life is dangerous," Jax replied. "Better to be inside the car then standing in front of it."

Simone laughed, tossing her head back slightly. "That's super dramatic. I like it."

She climbed into the driver's seat, re-buckling herself in as Jax did the same in the passenger seat. Carefully, she checked out all the controls and mirrors.

"Ready?" he asked.

She nodded quickly, but the butterflies in her stomach were swirling a million miles per hour. "I think so."

"The track is yours," he replied, gesturing toward the open track in front of them. "Go crazy."

Gripping the steering wheel tightly, she pushed the stuck shift into first, easing up on the clutch as she gently pressed her foot against the gas pedal, testing out the car's response. It slammed forward, intensely sensitive to the slightest pressure.

"Oh my God!"

Jax chuckled. "Relax. You've got this."

She swallowed, pushing down the nerves overwhelming her. She had this. Something about his confidence in her filled her with the same. If he knew she could do it...she could, she *would* do it. Not as gently this time, she pressed down on the gas and the car shot forward as she clutched and shifted through the gears as the engine revved to the correct sounds and speeds for each shift. She pushed down more, racing along the track at one of the fastest speeds she'd ever driven.

They started coming up on the first turn.

"Speed up around the turn. Really lean into it," Jax instructed.

"Faster?" Her eyes widened, already worried she'd go flying right off the track into the wall.

He nodded. "The curve will automatically slow you down. Speed up not to lose your momentum. The car will grip the track, so don't worry. Just go with it."

She turned the wheel as they maneuvered around the turn, pressing harder on the gas and shifting gears as they flew around the bend.

"Holy shit!" She gasped as they flew back onto the straightaway.

This was by far the biggest high she'd ever felt. All this power at her fingertips. Speed, energy, fuel...all of it in her control. The tiniest twitch of her hands could send the car veering off to the side, or the smallest push of her foot could bring them to a crashing halt. Everything was her choice... her decision.

"Ahh!" As they went around the second bend, Simone shrieked with excitement, overwhelmed at everything she was feeling.

Jax laughed, gripping the handle above his seat.

When they finally came to a stop at the beginning of the track, she just sat still for a moment, catching her breath.

"That. Was. Amazing," she panted. "Literally the most exciting thing I've ever done."

"And you didn't kill us," Jax added, unbuckling his seat-belt. "Come on. Let's go grab some dinner."

Her stomach growled. "Oh, that actually sounds perfect. I'm starving."

"I know a great place a couple miles from here, right on the beach." He climbed out of the car and she handed him back the keys as they walked toward the garage. "I think you'll like it."

Thirty minutes later, they were walking across the sand to a beachfront restaurant directly on the water's edge. The tide literally lapped at the guests' feet while they ate. How the entire place didn't just wash away, she didn't know.

"This is beautiful," she admitted, leaning down to pick up a pink seashell with stripes across the back.

"The shell?" he asked, leading her to their table and pulling out her seat.

"Well, that, too," she replied, taking her seat. "But I meant the restaurant. I've never been here before, but I love anything to do with the water."

"Sometimes living here, you don't get out and do the touristy things as often as you should." Jax took his own seat across from her. "Always be a stranger everywhere you go. You experience more from every place if you see it from foreign eyes."

Simone's lips lifted into a small smile, her elbows leaning against the table. "I like the way you talk. It's all philosophical quotes about life and living. Like you're one of the deepest thinkers I've ever met. You're not running or hiding from anything. You're just...living."

Jax reached his hand across the table, tangling his fingers through hers. "You sound like you have some experience with hiding."

She shrugged lightly. "Maybe a little bit. But it's not just me. Sometimes it's the people I meet." An image of Grant crossed her mind, and she felt a lump begin to swell in her throat at the thought. "Sometimes the people I meet are running, and I'm the one left behind."

He was quiet for a moment, then he squeezed her hand. "Anyone who'd leave you behind is a stupid son-of-a-bitch."

Simone laughed, covering up the small sob that almost choked through her. She took a deep breath and pushed away every thought of Grant and his stupid, beautiful blond hair and green eyes, or the way that he made her stomach tighten and her body ache. He was gone. He liked his freedom. He'd said so himself. Despite the fact that he'd still occasionally text her, she knew that she had to let go of this fantasy about him coming back for her.

He'd chosen not to be with her. He'd made his wants clear. She needed to respect that and stop holding out hope for something that wasn't in the cards.

Grant was gone, but Jax? Jax was here, and he wasn't going anywhere.

CHAPTER EIGHTEEN

"Honestly, what kind of bullshit is this?" Grant said into the phone.

Andrew let out a deep sigh from the other end. "I don't know what to tell you, Grant. We can't find her anywhere. The authorities are refusing to drop the charges against you until they speak with her and assess her involvement."

"Her *involvement?* She's the entire situation. I'm the one who isn't involved. Or at least, I shouldn't be."

"You can keep should-ing all over yourself, but that doesn't change the fact that without her confession, or a money trail, there's nothing we can do," his lawyer said. "You look guilty as sin."

"And the private investigator doesn't have anything yet?"

"Not yet. He says she's in America somewhere, so he's tailing her there. Now we just wait to find out what he uncovers. Maybe she'll come look you up because he did report that it doesn't seem like she's traveling with her partner anymore."

"Her partner? More like my ex-best-friend."

"Right, well...maybe they've parted ways," Andrew

surmised. "Infidelity never was the best foundation for a relationship."

Grant scoffed, because hell if that wasn't the goddamn truth. He wanted to wish her every misery in the world, but that would mean he'd still care about her, and truthfully, he didn't. He just wanted his name cleared and to be able to move on with his life without the threat of jail tailing him around the globe.

"When do you head back to Los Angeles?" the lawyer asked. "I have some paperwork to forward to your hotel."

"Two days." Grant hooked the phone between his ear and shoulder, freeing his hands to pour himself a glass of whiskey. His hotel room was a lot smaller in the middle of London, but he was still enjoying his time here. "Just for the live stream and an interview or two, then back here to London to complete this project."

"Where next after that?"

"New York." Grant took a sip from his glass. "It looks like I've got about six months on a Broadway show there. Might be nice to have some steady work and stay in one place for a while."

"You've got to be tired of all that jet setting at some point," Andrew mused. "I know I couldn't do it. I'd miss my wife too much."

"Not really a problem I have anymore," Grant replied.

"Right. Well...true."

"I'll call you when I'm back in the states, Wilson," Grant said, then took another sip from his glass. "In the meantime, send the paperwork to my London address."

"You've got it, Mercer." With that, the two men hung up the phone.

Grant sighed as he sat down in the leather armchair in one corner of his room. The last two months had been an insane amount of work between his legal battle and his current project. Now he was scheduled to go back to Los Angeles for the *Kiss Me, Kate* debut, and he was already feeling all sorts of apprehension about the prospect.

There was no doubt that he'd run into Simone again. Multiple times, probably. It was inevitable, and while a big part of him was looking forward to it, there was part of him dreading it as well. It was like ripping off a Band-Aid just to poke at the wound underneath. It was going to fucking hurt to see her and not be able to have her. Plain and simple.

Picking his phone back up, he typed her name in to his web browser's search bar. They hadn't spoken in almost two weeks, and even then, it had been sparse. The first month he'd been gone, they'd talked a lot more often. Phone calls, text messages, but then it had faded away. She'd stopped replying as often, and he got the hint. He stopped initiating, and when he did that, the conversation mostly faded away to nothing.

He didn't want to be upset about it, because technically that was the best thing for both of them. She needed to move on with her life as much as he did. But he'd be lying if he said it didn't hurt, if he said he didn't miss her...if he said he didn't still think about her every day.

Now here he was trolling the tabloids for any mention of her.

"What the fuck?" Grant suddenly sat up in his chair and scrolled through the web page he was on. There were at least five pictures of Simone on the beach in a skimpy bathing suit, her arms wrapped around the neck of a heavily tattooed, dark-haired man.

He knew he shouldn't look. Shouldn't torture himself. But he couldn't stop. He studied each photograph carefully —the way she smiled at him, the light in her eyes, the crooked way he grinned back at her. They were a fucking couple, and, damn it...they looked good together. They looked like they matched. Her tattoos complimented his, and the new blue streak in her hair even matched his eyes.

His stomach flip-flopped and churned as he exited out of the browser and tried to push the images out of his mind. *I don't care. I don't care. I don't care.* Hell, he'd keep repeating it to himself until it was true, and yet, he wasn't sure it ever would be.

Grant stood up and paced back and forth across his hotel room. He was going to be in Los Angeles and wound probably see the two of them together. No doubt, her boyfriend would accompany her to after parties and events related to the show's release. It didn't feel right.

She shouldn't be with him. Whoever this *him* was.

He swallowed hard as he realized that there was nothing more he really wanted than...her. And he'd already let her go.

Fuck.

CHAPTER NINETEEN

"I'M NOT NERVOUS!" Simone finished pinning her necklace around the back of her neck as she stared in the mirror in her dressing room.

Jax chuckled, leaning in behind her and kissing her shoulder. "That's my girl."

She warmed at his affection, melting backward into his touch. "Okay, I might be a little nervous. But not a lot. I've rehearsed a ton for today. I can't afford to be nervous."

They were only an hour away from the live performance of Kiss Me, Kate broadcast onto every television in the entire damn world. Nerves were to be expected, but she was a professional. She was trained and ready, and that was what she was going to depend on. She knew all her lines. She knew all her moves. She knew exactly what to do when.

Now she just had to do it.

Live.

In front of millions of people.

No big deal.

"I have no doubt that you'll blow them away," Jax said,

taking a seat on the couch to the far side of her dressing room. "I mean, you've already impressed the fuck out of me."

She and Jax had been dating for a couple weeks, but they'd been taking it pretty slow. While things with Grant had been hot and heavy out of the gate, she'd made sure to take her time with Jax. Honestly, she wasn't ready to jump into anything that fast right now. He was wonderful to her though, and somehow, he continued to be incredibly patient despite the fact that she'd barely done more than kiss him.

She checked her makeup again, even though her makeup artist had done an impeccable job and used a setter that would keep her makeup perfect for the entire performance.

"Ten minutes to set," a production assistant knocked on her door and announced.

Simone turned to face Jax. "This is it."

Jax stood back up and walked over to her, taking both her hands in his. "I'm going to be watching from the sides, baby. You're going to kill it."

She smiled, nerves scattering through her stomach. "Thank you, Jax."

They said their goodbyes as he began walking her back to set. When they were rounding the final corner toward the main stage, she ran directly into someone else walking the opposite direction.

She jumped back, nearly stumbling if not for Jax grabbing her arm to steady her. "Oh! Sorry!"

A startled Grant Mercer and his deep green eyes were staring back at her. His gaze darted to her left, scanning Jax, then back to her. "Simone..."

"Grant." She swallowed hard, suddenly more than aware of the awkward triangle she was in the middle of. "Uh, I didn't expect to see you here."

"They wanted me here for the performance," he replied, then he reached out a hand toward Jax. "Grant Mercer. Musical Director."

The two men shook hands.

"Jax Walker, Simone's boyfriend," Jax said with all the confidence she didn't have.

Simone coughed, surprised by the label he'd just given them. "Uh, right...well, I mean, we haven't discussed it. Uh, yes. So, there's that."

She closed her mouth, already wishing she could rewind her nervous ramblings. *Shit. Shit. Shit.*

Grant's eyes looked like they were pure fire, narrow and angry. "Yes. So, there's that." He turned back to Jax. "It was good meeting you, Mr. Walker. Simone, break a leg tonight."

With that, he walked past them down the hallway.

"Thank you," she called after his retreating figure.

Jax gave her a puzzled look. "What was that?"

She had zero idea how to answer that one, but *oh, that was just my ex-lover who I still think about all the time* seemed like a bad response. "Um, nothing? Come on. Let's go before we're late."

He nodded and followed her around the corner, but he still looked skeptical.

A few minutes later, they said their final goodbyes and she met with the rest of the cast on stage. As big as her final performance had been on *American Voice*—which was also broadcast on live television for millions to see—somehow this still felt bigger. It was a huge moment in her career, and if she pulled it off without a hitch, a lot of doors could open for her.

Her agent had been trying to land her the Broadway role, but without seeing the success rate of *Kiss Me, Kate,* the producers were reluctant. Tonight could be the final thing she needed to convince them that she could do the part—she could be *Anastasia*. The music in that play alone made her heart soar. She wanted to sing it on stage every night.

With only a few minutes left before the cameras started rolling, she slipped off to the side and grabbed a bottle of water, taking a few sips.

"Simone," a familiar voice at a near whisper came behind her.

She whirled around to see Grant only a few inches from her. God, he smelled so fucking good. All clean linen and something sweet she couldn't quite identify. His hair wasn't pulled back in a bun this time, falling down the sides of his face instead. She wanted to run her fingers through it and pull him to her, kissing him like they hadn't done when they'd said goodbye.

How she'd regretted never kissing him goodbye.

"Grant," she replied, barely above a whisper as well.

He bit his bottom lip, pulling at it slightly as his eyes grazed over her. "I'd wish you good luck, but you don't need it. You're amazing, Simone. You're going to be amazing."

He leaned in closer, his lips mere centimeters from hers.

She felt her cheeks heating, a blush crossing her face that she couldn't hold back. "Grant..."

"Tell me not to kiss you, Simone." His green eyes pierced through her, daring her.

A shiver ran through her, but she said nothing.

He closed the distance between them slowly, taking his time as his lips brushed hers. When they finally kissed, he lingered, and when they pulled apart, he sighed. Everything around them fell away for those few moments, and nothing existed but the way they breathed together.

"Grant," she whispered against his lips, though she didn't know what to say after that. Sadness hung over her like a thick blanket, and she could tell that he felt it too. "I have to go."

He stepped back, and with a small nod, walked back into the wings of the stage.

She stood there for another moment, trying to process what had just happened. But she didn't have the time. Pushing away the memories, the feelings, the stirring in her core, she returned to the stage ready to give the performance of a lifetime.

Tonight wasn't about Grant. It wasn't about Jax. It was about her.

CHAPTER TWENTY

"Congratulations!" Her sister, Aria, threw her arms around Simone the moment she stepped off stage at the end of the broadcast. "Oh my God, Simone. You killed it! That was spectacular!"

Simone couldn't stop smiling. The entire last two hours had been the high of her life, and she was still riding every thrill of it. "Thank you!"

"I know you told us not to come, but you also know we wouldn't listen." Aria pulled back to reveal the rest of her family behind her. Ben was holding Tillie, Teagan and Reed were there with Piper, and, of course, her mother was at the front of the pack. She never should have doubted that her mother would come, but with how little she'd been out since Jack's death, it had seemed unlikely.

"Baby girl," her mother gushed, her arms opened wide. "You were incredible. I never had any doubt but seeing it in person...wow!"

"Thanks, Mom," Simone replied, then finished her greetings with the rest of the family. "Thank you, everyone."

"Babe! That was amazing!" Jax rounded the corner and kissed her hard right on the lips.

Simone kissed him back, a little flustered at the public display, considering she hadn't said anything to her family about Jax yet. Teagan was the only one who knew they'd been seeing each other, but she'd sworn her to secrecy. There was no real reason why. For some reason, she just didn't want the world to know. She didn't want it to be so *real*.

"Uh, guys, this is Jax." Simone gestured between him and her family as he wrapped an arm around her back. "Jax, this is my family." She introduced everyone separately, and they all greeted him with open arms, but she could see their hesitancy. She doubted Jax could tell, but she knew her family. They weren't on board.

Her mother squeezed her hand. "Honey, show me where the bathroom is?"

"Sure, Mom," she agreed, leading her off the sides to a hallway that would lead to the bathrooms.

The moment they were alone, her mother began. "I don't see it, honey. I love you, but I don't see it."

"See what?"

"Jax." Her mother shook her head. "It's not like you not to tell us you're dating someone, first of all. Red flag."

"Nothing wrong with a little privacy," Simone argued.

"We've never done privacy in this family. Not from each other," her mother teased. "But what about Grant? I just saw him before the show started. He's here, and you two were so good together."

"Mom, he doesn't live here. He doesn't want a relationship with me."

Her mother scoffed. "Bullshit."

"Mom!" Since when did her mother curse like that?

Simone showed her into the bathroom and waited outside the stall while she used it.

"I'm just saying—the way Grant looks at you, the way he watched you tonight? That boy is not over you." Her mother washed her hands, giving her a hard look through the mirror. "Give the poor guy a chance."

Simone shook her head. "I'm with Jax now, Mom. I can't just give Grant a chance."

"You're young. Life is all about chances at your age."

They exited the bathroom and, thankfully, her mother dropped the conversation. It wasn't forgotten though. Even as she went through all the celebrations among the cast throughout the rest of the evening, she couldn't help but look for Grant in every crowd.

She didn't see him once though, and when it was finally time to head out for the night, she told Jax she was too tired and wanted to go home alone. He agreed, but she could see his disappointment.

Honestly, she was tired of disappointing him. She made a decision then and there that she was going to end things with Jax. He was sweet and wonderful, but there was just something missing that didn't excite her. He should. God, he should. Everything about him was thrilling and passionate and invigorating, and yet...she came up empty.

As she rounded the corner to her apartment, she came to a sudden stop. Grant was leaning against her doorframe. His eyes met hers, and he said nothing. They both just stared at one another for a moment.

Finally, she put one foot in front of the other and walked the rest of the length of the hallway. She pulled out her key and placed it in the lock, still saying nothing to him and refusing to look at him. The door swung open and she stepped inside, leaving room for him to follow her.

He closed the door behind him but didn't leave the entryway.

Placing her bags down on a side table, she finally turned around to face him. "What are you doing here, Grant?"

"I'm honestly not sure," he admitted, shaking his head. His perfect blond hair fell around his face, moving with him. "I couldn't not see you. Not tonight. Not after so many months apart."

"It hasn't been that long." Three months wasn't the end of the world, even though after he'd left, it sure as hell felt like it.

"Long enough for you to move on and find someone else." He raised his green eyes to stare at her. His comment was cutting, but his tone wasn't. It was full of remorse and sadness, and she wanted to put her arms around him and assure him...but how?

Simone shook her head. "That's not fair."

"I know." He stepped closer to her now, trailing his fingers down her arm. "But fuck, Simone...seeing him with his arm around you? Seeing you two in the tabloids all happy and smiling?" He put his hand on his chest, his expression twisted in pain. "I nearly broke."

"Is that why you're here?" she asked, her voice strengthening now. "Now that someone else wants me, you've suddenly realized you still want me? Do you really think that's fair?"

"It's the furthest thing from fair possible." Grant swallowed hard. "It's fucking bullshit, honestly. But just because I'm an asshole for showing up now doesn't make my feelings any less valid."

"Grant..." she began.

"Simone, these last few months apart didn't change anything for me," he said, cutting her off. "I still thought about you every day. I still wanted you. I've never stopped."

She scoffed, crossing her arms over her chest. "You *left*, Grant. Not only did you leave, but you made damn sure I knew before then that we were casual. We were *nothing*."

"We were *never* nothing." He grabbed her upper arms and pulled her body to his, their lips pressing together fast and hard.

He kissed her like he was starving and it was a stark contrast to the gentle and sweet moment they'd shared before the show. Her arms snaked around his neck, anchoring her to him as her knees shook and threatened to buckle. He wrapped his own arms around her waist and pinned her against him, devouring her mouth with every passing second.

Need built in her core, tension filling her body until she wasn't sure she could take it anymore. With a tiny hop, she bounced up and wrapped her legs around his waist. He held her, walking them toward the bedroom where they'd made love so many times before.

His knees hit the edge of the bed and they fell forward, collapsing onto the blankets while never once breaking their kiss. Her fingers slid through his hair, pulling him as close to her as they could possibly be. His hands hooked the bottom hem of her shirt and pulled it over her head, tossing it onto the floor. She shimmied quickly out of her jeans, then unhooked her bra, and rid herself of her panties. He undressed just as quickly and when they came back together, she relished the feeling of his hot skin pressed to hers.

"God, I've missed this, Simone," he whispered against her neck as he kissed, licked, and nibbled his way down to her chest. He cupped one of her breasts against one palm while his mouth took the other—slow, small circles of his tongue around her nipple before taking it between his teeth.

Simone cried out at the pinch of his bite, but her core tightened at the deliciously confusing sensation. Pushing her hips up, she moved against him, trying to satisfy the ache.

Grant's hand slid down between their bodies, dipping between her thighs and rubbing across her. She moaned against his neck, her face buried in the apex between his neck and shoulder as she clung to him. His member was hard and pushing against her thigh, but as much as she tried to move closer, he kept his distance.

With skilled fingers, he ran small circles around her clit. Her entire body shook and trembled with every second of contact, and then when he dipped a finger inside of her, she nearly exploded off the bed. Quick, deep thrusts of, first, one finger, and then two, he deftly hit the rough bundle of nerves inside her. Within seconds she was coming against his hand, crying out as she completely unraveled.

"I love feeling you come." His voice was husky and gravelly, and it danced across her skin like a rough whisper.

As the waves of her climax finally subsided, her need for him only grew rather than lessened. Her hands slid down his chest until she found his length, fisting her fingers around him.

"Fuck." Grant groaned, pumping his hips against her hand. "I need to be inside you."

"Yes..." She reached over into the nightstand next to the bed and pulled out a condom, handing it to him.

He made quick work of putting it on then returned to between her legs. Positioning himself at her entrance, he teased her at first. Small presses and circles until he finally slid inside in one long thrust.

"Oh!" Simone gasped, her fingers gripping his back as she held on.

With perfect rhythmic strokes, he slammed into her again and again until she could feel her second orgasm beginning to splinter inside her, teasing its imminent approach. Every move rubbed against her clit, stimulating her in every way possible until she wasn't sure she could take it anymore.

The way he looked at her, his gleaming emerald eyes hooded with desire, made her skin prickle with excitement. It was everything that they'd once been and more, as if not a second had passed since they'd last been together. She tried to push her thoughts away, keep her heart at bay, but it throbbed in her chest like a forgotten muscle she'd spent months ignoring.

One look from him, one touch, and she fractured open in every way.

"I'm going to come," she said, panting as she curled against his body. "Grant...oh, God..."

He gripped her hips, angling her higher so he pushed in deeper. His lips came down on hers, hard and hungry, absorbing every pant and moan as she finally came apart around him. Only moments later, she could feel him let go inside of her.

"Fuck..." He groaned, his forehead pressed to hers. "You feel so damn amazing around my cock."

She couldn't stop her grin. She'd missed his dirty talk, his lips, his dick...she'd missed all of him. As guarded as she'd tried to be the last few months, her heart was shattered open and stretched wide for him. She let out a deep sigh as he slid to the side and fell onto the mattress next to her. His arm wrapped around her waist, pulling her close to him.

"Grant...what does this mean?" she whispered, turning

her body to face his. Her arms were squeezed between them as he held her. "All of this."

His tongue slid across his lower lip. "I wish I could tell you that I put a lot of thought into this, but all I knew was that I needed to see you. I needed to be with you."

There was such intensity to his words, such honesty. Tears pricked at the corners of her eyes, and she swallowed hard in an attempt to keep them away.

"You needed to be with me for today?" she asked. "Or...forever?"

Grant pressed his lips to her forehead, kissing her. He was quiet for a few moments and her nerves went into over-drive with every second that passed.

"We tried casual, Simone," he began. "I don't think it worked. This doesn't feel casual. But...do you want to do long distance? I have to go back to London for a few weeks after this, and then I have a longer job in New York, but there are planes and video calls and other ways to still see each other. Is that something you're open to?"

Her heart leaped at his words. "I'm actually moving to New York for a role. Well, I'll find out this week for sure, but it's looking pretty likely."

He sat up, his eyes lighting up along with the smile on his lips. "Really?"

"And I don't mind long distance," she admitted. "I mean, it's not ideal and in the long term, I'd want to be *with* you, but...I'm willing to try if you are."

Grant wrapped his arms around her so tightly that it almost hurt. "Hell, yes, I'm willing to try."

She couldn't stop the tears this time from sliding down her cheeks. "We're really doing this."

He glanced down at her. "Are you crying? Babe..."

Simone laughed, which came out sounding more like a

choking sob since she was also crying at the same time. "I'm sorry. I know it's dumb. I'm just overwhelmed."

"It's not dumb," he replied, kissing her tears away. "I'm a little overwhelmed, too. I haven't done anything like this since...well, since my ex-wife. When that ended—damn, I was shattered. It's frightening thinking about putting myself out there again like that."

"I would never do what she did," Simone said. "Never. I promise."

He kissed her forehead. "I don't think you would. But... Jax? What's going to happen there?"

She shook her head. "That's nothing to worry about. I'd already decided earlier tonight to end things. We had never even talked about what we were."

"Good." Grant chewed on the corner of his bottom lip. "Shit, it kills me to think of you with him. With anyone." He rolled his body on top of hers, pinning her to the mattress. "This is all mine. You're mine."

Simone grinned, lifting her head and kissing him. "If it makes you feel better, I never slept with him."

Relief flooded Grant's expression. His lips crashed against hers and he reached over into the nightstand for another condom. "I need you right now."

She lifted her hips, pressing against his length. "I'm yours, Grant."

"All mine."

CHAPTER TWENTY-ONE

Grant's fingers slid across Simone's collarbone, then lower to her breast. He circled her nipple once, then twice. "Simone..." he whispered against her ear.

She stirred slightly from her sleep, leaning into his touch.

"Simone," he tried again, this time letting his fingers trail down her stomach to between her legs. "Wake up, beautiful."

"Mmm," she murmured, her eyelids fluttering slightly. Her legs parted, giving him access to every part of her.

His finger grazed her clit, rubbing slowly and firmly as her hips moved to meet him.

"Oh..." She moaned lightly, her eyes barely opening as she responded to his touch.

He loved seeing her like this—vulnerable and open. She was just rousing from sleep and yet, her body was wet and waiting. Everything about her—from the way her eyes were heavy with sleep to the way her nipples darkened with her arousal—made him know he'd made the right choice in coming here.

Hell, he hadn't known what he'd been thinking. It was insane to beg her to be with him when he had nothing to offer her—when she didn't even know his full story. He was being selfish. He knew that, and yet, he couldn't stop himself. He couldn't stop himself from wanting to be with her, wanting to touch her, wanting to claim every part of her as his own.

Why he hadn't done that months ago, he didn't know. Fear had let him almost lose out on the one woman who'd truly made him feel alive. Sure, he'd pretended that all the bucket list items they'd done together had been for her, but that wasn't the only reason. Everything about her made him want to really *live*. He'd spent so much of his life, of his marriage, just focusing on work. Maybe if he'd looked up every now and then, he never would have lost his wife. He'd pretended he'd been worldly, he'd had all these experiences and really lived, but until Simone came along, he hadn't even known the meaning of the word. He couldn't change the past, but he could vow to never make the same mistakes again.

He wouldn't allow his past to ruin this. Simone deserved more. She deserved the best he could offer her, and, damn it, somehow, he was going to give it to her.

"Oh, God..." She gasped as his finger slid past her clit and dipped inside her, teasing the bundle of nerves deep inside.

He leaned down and kissed her, soft and brushing as his lips caressed hers and pulled her awake with every stroke. Her body began to tremble and soon she was spasming against him as she moaned and came apart around his hand.

"Quite a way to wake up," she whispered finally, opening her eyes fully for the first time that morning.

"I let you sleep in," he teased, nodding toward the clock.

"But it's almost lunchtime, and your man is starving. Want to go get some food with me?"

She nodded, a big smile spreading across her face. "A man wanting to feed me? Hell, I could have another orgasm just from that."

Grant laughed then kissed her forehead. "You're ridiculous."

A loud knocking sound came from the living room, and they both glanced at each other for a moment.

"Did you order delivery?" Simone asked.

Grant shook his head. "Nope. I figured we'd go out. I don't know who it is."

She climbed out of bed and pulled on Grant's T-shirt that had been tossed to the floor the night before. "Weird. Let me go see."

"If it's some sales pitch, they better have brought breakfast," he called after her. He located his pants on the floor and pulled them on but then realized Simone was wearing his only shirt. "Shit."

Trotting out into the living room, he went in search of the rest of his clothes. "Babe, you've got my shirt."

He came to an abrupt halt when he saw Jax standing in the doorway...and he was kissing Simone. Her eyes were wide open and she looked almost as shocked as Grant felt.

"Uh..." Grant coughed, alerting them to his presence.

Jax broke the kiss, his gaze reaching Grant's, then slipping down to Grant's bare chest. He looked down to Simone's shirt—which was actually Grant's—then back to Grant. Recognition dawned in his expression and fury suddenly took over.

"Um...Jax, we need to talk," Simone started, trying to step back from him.

Jax grabbed Simone's wrist and yanked her toward him.

"Are you fucking kidding me right now? I put almost a month into this, and you just part your legs for the first dick to come along?"

"Ow!" She stumbled slightly, falling into him as she tried to extricate her wrist.

Grant leaped forward and stood directly in Jax's face, mere inches from him. "You have one second to let go of her before I knock you the fuck out."

Jax dropped her wrist but turned his fury toward Grant instead. He was at least three or four inches shorter than Grant, but he looked menacing as hell in that moment. "And who the hell do you think you are? You got a thing for sluts? Did you pay her? Is that the pussy magic I was missing—throwing a few dollars on the problem?"

Grant narrowed his eyes and grabbed the front of Jax's shirt, twisting his fist in the fabric. He lifted him straight off the ground and walked a few feet until they were standing in the apartment building's hallway. Placing him back on the floor, he gave him a hard shove until Jax fell backward. "If I ever see you near her again, I'll have you fucking arrested. Understand?"

With that, he turned around and headed back into the apartment, slamming the door behind him and making sure to lock it. "Fucking piece of work. I can't believe you dated that asshole."

His gaze settled on Simone and he realized that she was shaking and tears were sliding down her cheek. "Babe..." He wrapped his arms around her, lifting her up against his chest and carrying her back into the bedroom. "Don't cry. He's not worth it."

She shook her head, curling her body into his chest as they lay back down on the bed. "It's not that. It's just...how did I not see what kind of person he was? How did I not see he was only looking for one thing?"

"Men are dogs," Grant said.

"We only went out on like...three dates? Maybe four." She sniffed and wiped at her eyes. "I really didn't think it was that serious. I told him I wasn't ready for anything."

Grant kissed her forehead, gently stroking her back to comfort her as her tears began to slowly subside. "I'm sorry, babe. I mean, I'm glad as hell that he's out of your life, but I could seriously kill him for laying a hand on you."

"Thank you," she whispered softly after a minute. "For not killing him. A lesser man would have gotten in a fist fight or something. That wouldn't have solved anything and would probably get you arrested. What you did instead... that was a real man."

Pride welled in his chest at her compliment and how trusting she clearly felt. "Like I said, he's not worth it."

She nodded. "You're right. I don't know why I'm so upset. I was just so startled. The whole thing...it just caught me off guard."

He'd basically assaulted her, so Grant certainly wasn't surprised that she was emotional. Hell, he was still seething inside and wanted to run back out there and beat Jax to a bloody pulp. Piece of shit. He was damn lucky that Grant couldn't afford any run-ins with the law right now.

Damn lucky.

"Am I a terrible person?" Simone asked, barely above a whisper this time. "Do you hate me for being with Jax?"

Grant swallowed hard, considering her question for barely a second before responding. "Definitely not. Do I love the idea of you being with someone else? Hell no. Seriously, *hell no*. But we were broken up, and you had no reason to believe I'd ever be back. I admire you for being able to try and move on."

She trailed her fingers down the side of his face, gazing into his eyes. "I'm glad you're back, Grant. I...It wasn't the same without you. This is where I belong."

He brushed his lips across hers, kissing her gently. "I'm yours, Simone. I think I was the day we met. I think I always will be." His stomach suddenly growled loudly. "But also, can we please go get some breakfast? I might be dying of actual starvation."

Simone burst out laughing then sat up on the bed. "Come on. There's a cafe on the corner that has amazing breakfast sandwiches."

"God, that sounds so good right now," he said, climbing out of bed after her.

She giggled and swatted at his ass. "Such a simple creature," she teased.

"Food and sex, babe. That's all I need. Oh, and music." He counted off the three things on his fingers. "And now, you. Four things and I'm a happy man."

She slid out of his T-shirt and handed it to him, then went to go grab her own clothes. "What about back massages? I can't survive without a good massage."

He tapped his finger to his chin. "Does the massage lead to sex?"

She shook her head. "Nope. Just a massage."

"Then it doesn't make the list."

"You're ridiculous." She laughed again. "How did I get so lucky?"

Grant leaned over and kissed her on the top of her head. "I could ask the same thing."

"You CAN SEE the outline of my penis. And my balls." Grant crossed his arms over his chest.

Simone laughed, tilting her head to the side as she gazed at Grant's pelvis. He wasn't wrong. In the tight neon blue spandex outfit she'd made him wear, the outline of his package could be clearly seen. "Well, at least it's aerodynamic."

"What every man wants to hear about his penis," he replied. "You realize I'm going to fall and break my face, right?"

"This is super beginner aerial silk," she explained, even though she'd already told him all of this earlier. Clearly, he was not looking forward to these lessons, but thankfully, he'd been a pretty good sport about it so far. "I highly doubt they'll even have you off the ground on the first day."

"*First* day? I only agreed to do this once," he reminded her. "I'm not sure I could fit my balls into this outfit a second time. Literal blue balls, by the way."

Simone grabbed his arms, chuckling as she pulled him into the studio. "Stop being a big baby."

"Hard to do when I'm in a bright blue onesie."

Honestly, he looked amazing in spandex, mostly because she could see every rigid outline in his entire body. His muscles were prominently displayed, and Simone was struggling to keep her thoughts PG when she looked at him. Somehow, she'd convinced him to give aerial silk a try, and he was taking a beginner's lesson today. She was going to be joining in, even though she was far past the beginner's level.

"Hey, Nina!" Simone greeted the instructor when they entered the studio.

"Hi, Simone." Nina waved to her and walked over. "Is this your boyfriend?"

"Uh." Simone glanced at Grant. "This is Grant. He's my..." She honestly wasn't sure how to answer that question. They'd only gotten back together two days ago, and he was leaving for London again on Monday.

"Boyfriend," Grant finished the sentence for her. "Good to meet you, Nina. I apologize for my lewd outfit, but she made me wear it."

Nina's head tilted backward as she laughed at his response. "Spandex is what everyone wears to these classes, so don't worry. Baggier clothes get tangled in the fabric."

"See? I told you," Simone added, though she was still riding high from the fact that Grant had just called himself her boyfriend. I mean, it should be a small deal...but it wasn't.

The last few days had been a whirlwind and she was barely keeping up. Grant had assured her again and again that the incident with Jax wasn't her fault, and that he certainly wasn't upset by anything she'd done. Still, it had been hard to let go of the incident, or the guilt she felt around dating someone else while they'd been apart.

"We're going to start out on the mat, do some stretches,"

Nina explained, gesturing toward the mats underneath the silk hanging from the ceiling.

Simone's phone began ringing in her bag. "You guys get started without me. I'm just going to grab this really quickly."

Nina nodded and led Grant over to the mat.

Simone stepped out into the hallway and pulled out her phone. "Hello?"

"Simone, darling," Jasmine Rice, her agent, sang through the phone. "I have amazing news."

"The Broadway show?" She tried not to get her hopes up, but it was already soaring. Being a few days out from the live broadcast of *Kiss Me, Kate*, she was expecting to hear back any moment on the *Anastasia* role. "Did I get it?"

"You did, darling!" Jasmine sounded like she was clapping, even through the phone. "They want you in New York in two weeks to begin rehearsals. The show itself won't begin until the summer."

"Ah!" Simone screamed. "This is incredible!"

"You deserve it, Simone," her agent continued. "Your performance on *Kiss Me, Kate* is already receiving rave reviews. People are heralding you one of the greatest voices of the next generation."

Simone's cheeks heated at the compliment. "Well, that might be a bit of a stretch."

"It's not," Jasmine replied. "You're incredibly talented, and we need to plan out your next steps. You'll do *Anastasia* —I'm assuming you're saying yes?"

"Yes! Of course, yes!"

"Great. So, you'll do *Anastasia* until the end of the summer. Then we can aim for another show on Broadway, or another film? Or we can go on tour. You'll definitely have enough of a following by then to be able to sell out venues easily."

"On tour? I don't think people want to pay just to hear me sing..."

Jasmine scoffed. "Are you crazy? We're already getting offers for you to open for big names. You'll be the headliner in no time at all. We need to get started on recording an album."

Simone nibbled on her bottom lip, nerves building in her stomach. "Do you think I'm ready? I have a lot of songs I've written. They need some polishing, but I think I could do it."

"I'll set you up with a songwriter and the two of you can workshop what you've got," Jasmine replied. "But I have no doubt that you're ready. Let's aim for next summer to release your first album."

"One year..."

"You can do this, Simone," Jasmine assured her. "I wouldn't bullshit you."

That was certainly true. Jasmine Rice was one of the hardest working music agents in the business, and she definitely knew what she was talking about. With the success on *American Voice* and then *Kiss Me, Kate*, Simone knew she was positioned to launch a huge career. She just had to grab opportunity by the horns and ride it into her future.

"Thank you, Jasmine. I couldn't have done any of this without you." Simone glanced back through the window into the studio, trying not to laugh at the image of Grant with one leg up in the silk.

Damn, his penis really was on display.

"Not a problem, darling. I'll email you the details but start preparing for a move to New York! It looks like you'll be there a while."

Simone grinned. "I can't wait! My sister lives there, so I'll probably stay with her until I find my own place."

"Sounds perfect. Have a great day," Jasmine finished, saying goodbye before she hung up.

Simone tucked her phone back into her bag and then reentered the studio. Grant was face down on the mat with his legs up in the air, tangled in the silk.

"No, not like that," Nina was saying. "That's not even... No, I...Okay, let's just start over. I'm going to go grab a few more mats."

Simone tried not to laugh at Grant's clear failure as Nina walked off, but it was a losing battle. She burst out laughing, and Grant shot her an annoyed look.

"I can't feel my balls," he complained, falling onto the mat. He climbed back up to his feet, shaking off the silk. "Gracefulness is not my forte."

"Well, I was certainly enjoying watching," she teased.

Grant grinned, wiggling his pelvis. "Sure, you were. Who was that on the phone?"

"My agent, and guess what!" Simone clapped her hands together. "I got the Broadway role. I'll be in New York at least through the end of the summer."

"The same time I'll be there," he replied. "How serendipitous. Congrats, babe. That's amazing!"

"Thanks!" She wrapped her arms around his waist, leaned up on the tips of her toes, and kissed him. "I'm so excited. I've got to start packing and preparing to move."

"Let's just get a place together," he suggested.

"What?" She balked.

He shrugged, like it was no big deal that he was suggesting they move in together. "There's no point in us getting separate apartments while we're there because I definitely plan on spending every night with you."

Simone couldn't stop the smile from spreading across her face. "That sounds so...logical."

Grant chuckled but pulled her against his chest. "No, it sounds romantic. I don't want to be apart from you a moment more than our jobs already make us be. Hell, I'm climbing silk ropes with my balls hanging out for you, Simone. I think it's pretty obvious at this point that I'm falling in love with you."

She kissed him again, relishing the softness of his lips against hers. "I'm falling in love with you, too," she admitted.

"Good," he replied. "Because you're stuck with me. I'll have my realtor start looking for apartments in New York immediately."

"That sounds perfect."

"Any must-haves? Wood floors, giant closets, doormen?" he asked.

She shook her head. "I'm honestly fine with anything. Although...maybe it could be a pet-friendly building?"

"You don't have any pets," he pointed out. "Are we getting a dog?"

"I was thinking about it before all this happened." Honestly, she'd been wanting a dog for years, but she'd been putting it off because of how much responsibility she already had on her plate caring for her family. However, since she'd been focusing more on herself and making her own needs a priority, getting a dog seemed like the next best step.

"So, we're moving in together and getting a dog. No pressure," he teased. "Just promise me it won't be some little fluffy, prissy thing."

She grinned, having already been looking at pictures of little Shih-Tzus for weeks. "I can't make that promise."

"Oh, good Lord," he muttered. "All right. Let's do this. Want to go to the shelter after this?"

Her heart sped up, and she jumped up into his arms. "Yes!"

Grant laughed, catching her and swinging her around in a circle. "I can't even believe my life right now."

"Are you happy?" she asked, because she was feeling deliriously so. The man she was starting to fall in love with was giving her everything she'd ever wanted.

Commitment and a dog? Jackpot.

CHAPTER TWENTY-THREE

"SHE IS the sweetest little thing I've ever seen," Teagan admitted, cuddling the small fluffy white puppy that Simone and Grant had adopted last week before Grant had left for his last two weeks in London. "What's her name again?"

"Mildred. Or Millie." Simone handed her a blueberry and the puppy mashed it up quickly.

Teagan chuckled. "You know that name is ridiculous, right?"

"Yep!" Simone didn't care one bit. She loved people names for dogs, and it perfectly fit hers. Grant had balked slightly at how tiny and fluffy the puppy was, but after some cajoling, he'd fallen just as in love with Millie as Simone had.

"Did you guys pick an apartment yet?" her sister asked. "You know which one I'm rooting for."

She'd shown her sister the options they were looking at, one of which was on the same block as Teagan's, so of course she wanted her to pick that apartment. "We signed the lease yesterday—and yes, it's for the one by you. Luckily, that's also super close to the theatre, so I can walk to work."

Teagan pumped a fist in the air. "Yes! Free babysitting!"

Simone laughed and shook her head. "I didn't agree to that!"

"Like you could resist Piper's little face," Teagan replied, then ran her hands over her belly which was getting larger and larger with every passing day. "Or whoever this little face is going to be."

"I am glad I'll be there when you have the baby," Simone admitted. She definitely wanted to be around for the birth of her next niece or nephew, and she was thrilled that the entire family now knew about Teagan's pregnancy. Honestly, it was pretty impossible to keep hidden at this point since she was so clearly pregnant. "And, of course, I'll babysit when I'm not working. During the show's run, though, I'll be doing eight shows a week. Six days—two on Saturday, and two on Sunday."

"I know that schedule all too well," Teagan admitted, no stranger to Broadway herself. "It'll be killer for those few months, but you won't regret it."

Teagan was now working on a dance film that she was going to be starring in—her first solo film without Reed. Her career had risen with the *Break Down* series she'd done with Reed, but it had taken off on her own now. She was one of the most famous dancers both in Hollywood and on Broadway and making use of every second of her fame. She was even hosting a dancing competition show with a million-dollar prize, and it was clear that she was one of the most respected dancers in the industry. The pregnancy had forced her to take a temporary pause, but she was still just as hot a commodity.

"I'm definitely nervous but looking forward to it."

Simone picked up Millie from the floor and cuddled her in her lap.

"I still can't believe you two are moving in together," Teagan continued. "You realize you two barely know each other, right?"

Simone shrugged. "We know enough. And what we don't know, we'll learn. It's not like we wouldn't have spent every night with each other anyway."

"I guess that's true," Teagan agreed. "I mean, financially, New York is impossible without a partner or a roommate. Though, I've seen your check for the play, and girl...I'm jealous as fuck."

Simone laughed. "What? Why?"

"You're getting lead role money!" Teagan shook her head, as if she didn't know what it was like to be rolling in dough. Between her multiple salaries and Reed's paychecks, she made more than Simone could imagine. "It took me like three shows to get to that level."

"Well, I'm twenty-six. It's about time I start making a decent paycheck after living off Mom and Dad for the last two decades," Simone countered, because honestly, all of her gigs had barely paid out until now. Despite the fame *American Voice* had given her, she hadn't won and therefore —no prize money. *Kiss Me, Kate* had been a nice paycheck, but they'd vastly undersold her and she knew it. It'd been worth it, however, to break into the field and get her name out there. "Dad would be thrilled that I'm finally out of the house."

Teagan chuckled lightly, barely audible. "He loved having you there, despite all his complaining."

Simone nodded, because she knew that, too. A sigh rose heavily in her chest. "I miss him."

"Me, too," her sister agreed. "I'm thrilled to see Mom doing so much better, though."

"Is she?" Simone tilted her head to the side, because honestly, she couldn't tell. Sure, her mother got out of the house more, but their home was still a shrine to her father, and she visited his grave every morning. "It doesn't really feel like she's moved on."

"I don't think she ever will," Teagan replied. "Part of me thinks she shouldn't. Dad was her great love—her everything. I don't know if there is anything after that. She's holding on to those memories, that connection, but at least now she's making room for other people in her life. She's coming out to dinner and seeing all of us girls regularly. I think that's the most we can hope for."

Simone was quiet for a moment, gently petting a now snoring Millie. "Do you think that's really how it works? You get one great love, and then that's it?"

Teagan shrugged, though her face seemed convinced. "I don't really know, but if Reed died tomorrow? God forbid." She made the sign of the cross over her forehead and chest. "That would definitely be it for me. I couldn't date again. I couldn't love another man. Reed is...he's the air I breathe. I couldn't imagine breathing in anyone else."

Simone leaned back against the couch cushions, thinking about her sister's passionate response. Did she feel that way about Grant? Was he her everything? "I really want to feel that way. I want that kind of intensity," she admitted aloud.

"Maybe you and Grant will have that. Sometimes love is a slow burn."

Simone shook her head. "I don't think we're a slow burn. We...fit. Like, when he's here with me, everything just seems right. It just seems to belong. It's comfortable and happy and like...my missing piece."

Teagan smiled and nodded her head. "That's all love is—finding the match that makes you whole."

"I don't know if it's love..." Simone swallowed hard, the very word making her stomach turn and nerves bloom up inside her even though she knew it was. "That just seems like a lot to admit out loud."

"You're psyching yourself out," her sister replied. "You've always struggled with trust—especially with men. Remember Peter? You were looking for reasons not to trust him from the start, and when he confirmed that he wasn't trustworthy, you just shut yourself off for good after that."

"What?" Simone blinked...hard. Was that true? "I didn't shut myself off."

"He's literally the last person you dated before Grant, and that was years ago."

Simone considered her sister's observation, and honestly...she wasn't that far off base. She had kept to herself for quite some time after Peter and stumbling into this relationship with Grant had been purely accidental and very unlike herself. Hell, she'd even kept herself closed off with Jax, taking things much slower with him than she'd let things go with Grant.

"I'm just saying," Teagan continued. "I wouldn't put those fears on Grant. He seems like a really great guy and he genuinely cares about you. You keep talking about wanting to experience this 'great love,' but I think you already are. You just need to open yourself up to it."

Simone nibbled on the edge of her bottom lip. "Shit. You're right."

Her mind swarmed through every memory of their time together. The back booth at the speakeasy. The picnic behind the Hollywood sign. Waking up in bed together to his arms wrapped around her. How ridiculous he looked trying aerial silk for the first time. The way he looked at Millie the first time he saw her fluffy little face. The fire in his eyes when he'd seen Jax grab her wrist. The way he knew exactly what her body wanted at every moment.

The feeling of warmth and happiness in her chest at every memory. The smile that spread across her face when she pictured his face and the way his beautifully accented voice said her name. Good God...

I'm in love with Grant Mercer.

CHAPTER TWENTY-FOUR

It had been exactly one week since Simone had come to the realization that she was head over heels in love with Grant. He was due back from London any minute, and she was waiting for him at their new apartment in New York City with Millie roaming around her feet, sniffing every inch of the new space.

Simone walked around the interior, but it was stark empty. There was no furniture at all except a few suitcases that she'd brought with her from Los Angeles. Their bed was supposed to be delivered this afternoon, and the rest of their furniture and the things from her apartment in Los Angeles would be trickling in throughout the week.

She'd hired an interior decorator to help her put the space together because, honestly, she didn't have that creative eye to do it herself. And their first apartment together needed to be perfect. She wasn't sure why she felt that way, but there was just this pressure building up in her every second since she decided that yes...she was in love.

Because that's what love was...a decision.

Sure, the feelings had been seeping into her soul ever

since she'd met Grant, but she'd kept them at bay. She'd withheld diving in headfirst, and then last week...she dove. There was no turning back now—it was sink or swim. And she liked that. She liked that she was in control. She had chosen, and this was her choice. There was something so safe about that, about knowing that this was what she wanted—*he* was what she wanted—and now she had that.

She walked over to the kitchen and opened the fridge. They might not have any furniture, but she'd stuffed the fridge with all their favorite foods and Grant's favorite beer. She pulled a bottle out and unscrewed the top. Taking a long swig of the cold, hoppy brew, she swallowed it down and let out a loud sigh. It was the perfect treat after lugging all her things up here this morning. Okay, the doorman had helped, but still. Beer and moving—it just went together.

Her thoughts were suddenly interrupted by a knock at the front door.

Simone jumped, startled by the sudden sound. "Millie, Daddy's here!" she said excitedly, rushing for the front door. The puppy circled around her feet, almost tripping her, but Simone hopped over her deftly.

She swung open the door, then paused. It wasn't Grant at all, but rather a ridiculously tall, statuesque redhead, who might be one of the most gorgeous women Simone had ever seen. Hell, she wouldn't be shocked at all if the woman was a model, because...damn...she was freaking perfect.

"Uh, hi," Simone greeted her, keeping Millie back from running out the front door by blocking her with her feet. "Can I help you?"

The woman looked confused to see her, as if she was expecting someone else. "Yeah...I'm looking for Grant? Grant Mercer?"

"He's due back any minute," Simone replied. "Is there something I can do for you?"

The woman shook her head. "No. Are you..." She narrowed her eyes. "Are you the maid or something?"

Simone stood up straighter. What the hell? "No. I live here."

The woman looked even more confused, scanning her up and down like she was on the sales rack at a discount clothing store. "So, *you're* dating Grant?"

What the hell were these questions? "Not really sure how that's any of your business, but yes."

She might not be a model-beautiful like this woman, but she looked damn good enough to date Grant. The fact that this woman might be implying otherwise was about to get her a ton of sass and possibly a slap across the face.

"Wow." The woman looked taken aback and...a little sad? She tossed her red hair over her shoulder, shrugging lightly. "I'm surprised anyone would date a guy facing ten years in jail. Though, I guess it helps his image. Either that, or he's living off your paycheck."

Simone's eyes widened. "Excuse me?"

That was a hell of a lot of information thrown at her at one time.

A wicked grin spread over the redhead's lips. "Oh. You didn't know? That makes sense now. Grant was never a great communicator when we were married either."

Married? This was the ex-wife? What the actual fuck.

"You're...you..." Simone shook her head, taking a deep breath. *Don't pass out.* "Why are you here?"

Simone certainly didn't know the full story of their divorce, and clearly there was a lot that she didn't know about. Ten years in jail? What the hell kind of bomb drop was that? Grant had never mentioned legal troubles once, and she'd certainly never heard him talk about a lawyer or a criminal trial or anything of the like.

She wasn't about to let his ex-wife see her crack though. *Hold it together.*

"Don't worry about it, sweetheart. I'll check in with Grant later." With that, the beautiful bitch walked back down the hallway, got on the elevator, and left.

Simone stared after her, then slowly retreated inside their large penthouse apartment that suddenly felt too small. The walls were closing in on her, and she couldn't breathe. Returning to the kitchen, she downed the last of her beer and cracked open another one.

An ex-wife who looked like she could be on the cover of Vogue.

A possible jail sentence...for what?

So many secrets.

Simone nibbled on the edge of her lip, trying to wrap her mind around everything she'd just learned. Why hadn't Grant told her? Why hadn't he confided any of this with her? Was he about to leave again? This time for jail?

What about his money troubles? Did he even have those? She'd been the one to pay the down payment on their new apartment, and he'd planned to pay her back his half when he returned to the states. At least, that was what they had discussed. But had he planned on it?

Was he using her as some kind of good-boy image to get out of jail? Or using her for her money? It wasn't until recently that she'd had more money than she knew what to do with, so she certainly hadn't expected that to be something a man would use her for.

It was beginning to sound frighteningly like her ex-boyfriend, Peter using her for her connections. She'd sworn she would never let that happen again. She'd never be used and lied to.

Yet, here she was.

Did she trust the wife? Was it all a lie?

Shaking her head, she slid down to the tile floor in the kitchen and sat with her back against the cabinets. "What. The. Hell."

Millie rubbed her face against her leg, falling over her shin and falling asleep between her legs. Simone downed the rest of her second beer, opting to stay on the kitchen floor.

"Simone?" A knock came on the front door as it was pushed open. Grant's face appeared as he walked in, dropping a few bags on the floor by the front door. "Why isn't this door locked? We live in New York City now, babe. You need to stay safe. Where are you?"

She lifted a hand and waved so he'd spot her over on the kitchen floor. "Here."

Grant chuckled, walking over to her. "What are you doing drinking on the floor?"

"Trying to decide whether or not I'm dating a liar."

His brows furrowed, his arms crossing his chest. "I feel like I'm missing something."

"Your ex-wife just paid us a visit," Simone continued, pushing up off the floor and going over to the fridge for a third beer. She popped the top and turned to look at him.

His eyes widened.

"She...she did?" He cleared his throat. "What did she say?"

"Why are you worried about what she said?" Simone felt her jaw tightening as her teeth ground together. *That* was his first question? Wondering if she kept his story straight? "What do you think she said, Grant?"

"Well, I think she clearly said something that pissed you off, and considering how much bad blood is between her and I, it could really be anything." Grant took a deep breath. "There's a lot about my past we haven't talked about yet, Simone."

"I'm gathering that after our conversation. How about you enlighten me?"

"Serena and I were married for five years. Together for almost eight," Grant began. "Everything was great between us at first, but while I was happy to just work and live my life with her, she always wanted more. She was always chasing the next big thing—the next adventure."

Simone took a few more gulps of her beer. To be fair, the bombshell who'd shown up at their door certainly did look like the type to chase glitz and glamour.

"My best friend at the time...he was a thrill seeker too, and they hit it off—unbeknownst to me. They ended up running away together, and so...we got divorced."

She shook her head. "I'm sorry that happened, Grant, but I feel like I already know that story."

"Right." He shifted his weight from one leg to the other, then finally blew out a deep breath. "But she didn't just leave me. She took everything we had. Every dime. Emptied all of our accounts while I was on a trip one week, and by the time I came home and tried to repair the damage, she was gone with everything I owned."

That certainly could explain the financial problems.

"As if that wasn't bad enough, she emptied our business accounts, embezzling hundreds of thousands from companies we were on the boards of." Grant's face darkened, his eyes shifting to the ground. "She used my accounts, my passwords, my everything. Every paper trail shows it as me who took the money. That's why there is currently an arrest warrant out for me if I try to set foot back in New Zealand."

This made absolutely no sense. "So why not just turn her in?"

"Without a confession from her, I have no proof." Grant shook his head. "There's nothing I can do but avoid New Zealand and pray that my private investigators can find the evidence needed to prove it wasn't me."

The situation sounded dire as hell, but she still couldn't wrap her mind around the fact that he'd never told her any of this. They'd been together for several months now, longer if you didn't count the break in the middle. This kind of information should have come up to begin with, not when it was forced out of him by a surprise visit from the woman who was apparently destroying his life.

"You look like you don't believe me," Grant observed, stepping closer to her and running his hands down her forearms. "Simone..."

She shook her head and pulled her arms away from him. "Don't. I...Grant, this is a lot. And you're choosing *now* to tell me. When you're forced into it. You didn't bring this up once on your own."

"I agree that it's not ideal, but how do you really talk about something like this?"

She tossed up her hands. "You just say 'hey, Simone, I've got some super shitty stuff to tell you about my ex-wife and my potential jail time.' Literally, that's it."

He bit his bottom lip, swallowing hard. "You're right. I should have told you."

She stared at him, not sure what to believe. Hell, she wanted to believe his story, but he'd kept this part of his life from her. He'd hidden that, so how did she know he wasn't hiding more? How did she know that Serena's vague version of events wasn't the truth? The woman was apparently guilty of hundreds of thousands of dollars of embezzlement, but just showed up at their door? How'd she even get their address? How could she risk showing her face?

"Honestly, Grant...I don't know what to believe right now." She placed her beer down on the kitchen counter. "I'm going to take Millie and go stay at Teagan's."

"Simone, don't do that. Let's talk about this." He ran his hands up to her shoulders and tried to pull her closer to him, but she wiggled free and took a few steps back.

"What else is there to talk about? Is there more I don't know?"

He shook his head. "No, that's everything."

"Then I need time to think. You kept this from me. For months, Grant. Months."

Grant's expression dropped, a hopelessness passing over his eyes, but he didn't reply.

"And I don't know if you ever would have told me," she continued. "There's a lot you need to resolve in your life, and you let me sign a lease with you without ever bringing it up. You know what it feels like, Grant?"

Grant still didn't respond.

"It feels a lot like I'm being used. Maybe for the rent, maybe for the image—I don't fucking know. Either way, it feels a lot like you've got an entire life I'm not a part of. Maybe you never planned for me to be."

"That's not true," he answered. "I would have told you."

"Eventually?" Simone shook her head, grabbing her keys and wallet from the counter. "I can't know that now, can I?"

She scooped Millie up in one arm and headed for the front door.

"Simone, don't leave. Don't do this. I just got back—we haven't seen each other in two weeks."

That was another aspect of this that pissed her off. Today was supposed to be for celebrations and kisses, not ex-wives and bombs dropped. "You've got some things you need to figure out, Grant. Deal with your situation, and then maybe we can talk."

With that, she left.

CHAPTER TWENTY-FIVE

"Well, shit." Andrew sighed into the phone. "That's quite a fuck up, Mercer. I'd leave your ass, too."

Leaning against the kitchen counter, Grant swirled the whiskey in his glass and then sipped.

Despite the fact that Andrew worked for him, the two were close friends. If Grant was being honest, his lawyer might actually be his only friend. That realization hit him harder than he even realized, because that shouldn't be the case. Simone should be the one who knew all his secrets, the one he confided in. Instead, his old, surly lawyer was the person he turned to for everything, the only person who actually knew all his demands and was helping him try to tame them. Part of it was necessity, but it wasn't a good excuse, and he knew that now.

"I'm beginning to see that," Grant admitted, taking another sip.

He glanced around the mostly empty apartment—only a newly delivered bed in the bedroom and a single chair in the living room. It had been a full day since Simone had left, and he'd tried both texting and calling but gotten no response.

He could just show up at her sister's apartment, but that seemed too invasive. She wanted her time away, space to think, and he wanted to give that to her. But fuck, it was hard not to just march over there, toss her over his shoulder, and drag her home. She belonged here, with him.

"She has a point though," Andrew continued. "You've got shit you need to deal with. You can't just be on the run from an entire country forever, Mercer."

"It's worked so far." Grant rubbed his hand across his chin, the stubble of his sleepless night already appearing across his jaw.

"It's not a permanent solution, and you know that. What happens when you want to get married or buy property or do anything that requires you not to be a fucking fugitive?"

He knew his lawyer had a point, but it was hard as hell to admit it. "There's *nothing* the investigators have come up with? I mean, she was here, Andrew. She showed up at my apartment."

"They're closing in," he admitted. "They think they have a hotel where she's staying, but it appears she's alone. If they can find what money she is using and trace it back to the serial numbers on the stolen cash, then we might be able to convince a judge. In the meantime..."

"I'm still a fugitive."

"Yep," his lawyer confirmed. "We might be able to gain favor by working with law enforcement."

Grant swallowed hard. "You mean...turning myself in?"

"It's not ideal, but it's also not forever. At least, we'll work as hard as we can to make sure it's not forever."

He shook his head then swallowed the last of the amber liquid in his glass. "And if we can't find the proof of my innocence? Then I just go to jail for ten years. Maybe more?"

"That's a risk we'd be taking," Andrew admitted, his tone heavy. "It's a really shitty risk."

Grant walked over to the liquor cabinet and pulled out the sole bottle of whiskey, pouring himself another glass. This was what Simone had been talking about—him running and hiding from his problems. By not talking to her about them, he'd been trying to hide, act like they didn't even exist, like everything was fine.

He hated that he'd lied to her. Every day that went by that he didn't tell her, it felt like his problems were further and further away. She made him so happy, feel so free. She made him forget. But she was right—he should have told her. He should have invited her into his whole life—the good and the bad.

"I don't know if I can trust the system not to fuck me over, Andrew," Grant replied. "They haven't found anything so far. I am literally still looking at serious jail time."

"Mercer, I promise you that I'm doing everything I can on my end to find your ex-wife and prove her involvement here, but I can't guarantee that I'm going to be successful. All I can tell you is that I'm going to never give up until you're free—on paper and in person."

Grant nodded his head, sipping at his second glass. "I know, Andrew. I know you're doing your best. But...you're right. It's time to stop running. It's time to stop hiding."

"What are you saying?"

He took a deep breath, slowly expelling it from his lungs. "Double the pay for the private investigators and ask them to double their hours. Do anything we can to light a fire under their asses. Then, book me a flight to New Zealand."

"Are you sure about this?"

He wasn't sure about anything right now, but all he did know was that he was tired of embezzlement charges hanging over his head. He could spend the rest of his life running, or he could face it head-on and hope that justice would prevail.

"I'm sure," he replied.

He didn't know what this meant for him and Simone, but he knew that they didn't have a chance at anything if he was always running from his past. If he wanted to truly beg her forgiveness, if he wanted to truly prove to her that he was ready to start fresh with her and leave the past behind them, then he needed to do exactly what she'd said. He needed to deal with his situation.

"You've got it, Mercer. I'll be there when you land. We're going to fight this. We're going to fight like hell."

Grant had no doubt that his lawyer would be by him every step of the way. "Thanks, man. Things are about to get rough."

He just hoped he was strong enough to handle it.

CHAPTER TWENTY-SIX

"You just left?" Teagan's eyes widened from across the breakfast bar in her high-in-the-sky New York apartment. "Like, permanently?"

"I don't know," Simone admitted. "I didn't really think that far ahead."

After having moped around on her sister's couch for several days, Teagan had finally forced her to explain what had been going on between her and Grant. She'd been reluctant to share at first because she didn't want to tell them about Grant's legal troubles, but Teagan had refused to let her stay silent about it for another moment.

Teagan leaned back in her seat, shaking her head. "Shit. That's a lot to deal with. I don't even know how he kept that from you, honestly. How does he ever plan on going home? Or is New Zealand just off limits for the rest of his life? Can't they force him to come back?"

She shrugged, because honestly, she had no clue. New Zealand law enforcement wasn't really her specialty, and it was certainly an odd situation. "I have no idea what his plans are. All I know is that I'm not going to be a part of it."

"Do you really think that's fair, though?" Teagan chewed on the edge of her lip for a moment, then swirled her spoon around in her cup of tea. "I mean, you two are together, right?"

"We are. Or we were." She really didn't know what they were.

"Then you go through these trials and tribulations together. You support one another through the hard times."

Teagan had a point, but Simone didn't think it really applied here. "Sure, if you're both on the same page and walking in eyes open. He may never have even told me about this if his ex-wife hadn't. She told me he was probably using me for my image or my money."

Her sister shook her head. "I honestly don't see that being the case. Not with Grant. He really doesn't seem the type. And he's getting paid any day, if not already, for *Kiss Me, Kate*. Plus, he's got the London project. The man has money."

That part was definitely true. Even if he had nothing at the moment, there was no doubt he had a few large paychecks coming in soon. He was still one of the best in his field, and that didn't come at a small price tag.

"So, then what? Why not tell me?"

Teagan shrugged this time. "Embarrassment? Protecting his own image? Being a stupid man like the rest of them?"

"I can't handle liars, Teag." Simone shook her head. Whether he was using her or lying to her, neither option seemed good. "What else don't I know?"

"That's fair," her sister admitted. "Lying is...it's toxic. It erodes trust, and now you're left wondering whether you can trust anything he says or has said."

"Exactly."

"But...I don't know, Simmy. It just seems like leaving is a

pretty dramatic response." Teagan took another sip of her tea. "Relationships are hard. People fight. People lie. People forgive."

"We've barely just started our relationship, though. Who's to say this isn't a sign of what's to come? Who's to say that he doesn't plan on lying about more things in the future?"

"That's the risk that comes in every relationship," Teagan replied, leaning forward and rubbing the top of Simone's palm. "There's always a risk of being hurt, of the bond being broken. But think about the Grant you know— the man you *know*. Can you trust him? Can you feel that innate sense of who he is?"

Simone swallowed hard, thinking back to every moment she'd spent with Grant. All the sleepless nights curled around each other in bed, the whispered stories and truths shared in pillow talk, the fun adventures and new experiences handled head on, hand-in-hand. Despite the pull of fear yanking at her heart, she did *know* him. She did know that he was a good man at his core. She still didn't understand why he'd lied, but she knew from the dozens of apology texts and voicemails on her phone right now that he was sorry. He did care.

If it came to believing him or the ex-wife who'd shown up at their door, who should she believe? The answer hit her without a doubt.

Grant.

"I should talk to him," Simone finally replied with a deep sigh. "At least give him the chance to apologize."

"See how you feel after that, because I'd be willing to bet you'll forgive him." Teagan squeezed her hand. "I'd be willing to bet you already have."

Simone gave her sister a small smile. "When did you get so wise?"

Her sister laughed, shaking her head. "Not wise, but I do know a thing or two about forgiving a stupid, stupid man."

Laughter bubbled up between them as Simone thought of the fact that Teagan had had to forgive her now-husband, Reed, for the biggest betrayal of all—leaving her at the altar. Compared to Reed's crime, Grant's lie seemed like nothing.

Simone realized she had probably been dramatic about the entire thing, but she had needed to get away to think about it all and decide how to get past it. How to forgive. Relationships were new territory for her, and trusting? Shit, that was the hardest part.

Taking a deep breath, she pulled out her cell phone and opened the text thread between her and Reed. There were several missed texts from him apologizing and begging her to come home.

I need to talk to you. It's urgent.

His last text was sent yesterday, but she still hadn't replied to him. She'd been gone almost three days now, most of which she'd spent moping on her sister's couch. Taking a deep breath, she hoped she wasn't too late, or that he hadn't given up on them yet.

She typed out a quick response and hit send before she could change her mind.

I'm coming home.

She waited for the text bubble to pop up, indicating that he was trying a response, but nothing came. She wasn't sure why she'd expected him to respond so quickly, but she suddenly felt a moment of panic, an urgency that told her she was missing something. She was missing him.

"I'm going to go." Simone looked up at her sister. "Can I leave Millie here for the night?"

"Sure!" Teagan ruffled the fur on top of the puppy's head where she sat at their feet chewing on a large dog bone. "I love my new little fur-niece."

"Thanks," she replied, grabbing up her purse and keys. She was in a cab within five minutes on her way back home. Dread swirled in her stomach, but she couldn't pin point why. She just suddenly felt this fear and couldn't seem to push it away as hard as she tried.

It wasn't about talking to Grant. Somehow, she thought that conversation would actually go okay, but...there was still something nagging at her.

Her phone rang, and Grant's face popped up on the screen. His long hair was pushed behind his ears, his smile stretching across his face as he stared back at her. It was a picture she'd taken of them at the beach, and the carefree happiness in his expression was a moment she wanted to return to so badly.

She clicked the answer button. "Hello?"

"Simone." His voice was gravelly and dark, an ominous tone that matched the nerves pitting in her stomach. "You answered."

"I'm in a cab on my way home," she replied. "I think we should talk. I'm ready."

A sigh came through the phone. "I'm not at our home."

Our home. Her heart pumped harder at the reference.

"Oh. Well, when will you be home?" she asked, chewing on the edge of her thumb. Nerves wracked her stomach because she could just tell...there was more to this story.

"I'm...I'm probably not coming home. Not anytime soon, at least."

She swallowed, trying to understand how things had

gotten so out of control. One argument and their relationship was over? "Oh."

"It's not like that." He sighed again. "I just landed in New Zealand. I'm still on the plane, but as soon as I step off...I'm going to be arrested."

Her eyes widened, her free hand gripping the worn leather seat of the taxi cab. "You—You're in New Zealand? Wh—Why?"

"As much as I hate to admit it, you were right. I've been running from this for too long, hiding it from you and everyone. It's time to face it head on."

The turning in her stomach switched from unknown nerves to full blown panic. "Grant, no. You can't! You don't know how long you'll be detained. What if there's no way to free you?"

"I'm confident in my men. They're looking for proof, and they'll find it." He paused for a moment, and her heart ached with the silence. "Eventually."

Sobs began to build in her chest, bubbling up her throat. "Grant...you can't do this. You can't leave me like this."

"I'm *not* leaving you," he promised. "Sweetheart, I love you. I'm sorry that it is taking a moment like this for me to tell you, but I love you with everything in me. I'm doing this for us. We can't start our future when the past is holding me hostage."

She shook her head, even though he couldn't see her. "I love you, too. I'm so sorry I walked out. I'm sorry I got so upset."

"Don't be. You had every right to be upset. I'm sorry I lied. I'm sorry I withheld a part of myself. I don't want to ever do that again."

He sounded so strong, so assured, and she didn't know how that could even be possible. In a matter of minutes, he'd be taken into custody. Jail. Prison. She didn't know. She didn't know what would happen to him. Hell, he didn't know either.

Fury built inside of her at the thought of his ex-wife. Serena. *Fuck her.* This was all her fault. "Is there anything I can do, Grant? I want to help. Let me help." This was all her fault. "Please."

He was quiet for a moment, then his voice came through softly. "This is my battle, Simone. I don't want to burden you with it. I'll take care of this, and then—if you're open to it—I'll come back to New York. I'll come back to you."

She bit her bottom lip, trying to hold back a cry. "I'll be here. I wish you could just turn around and come back."

"Part of me wishes I could, too. But I have to do this." He went on to explain a few logistics, how he'd paid the penthouse in full for the next year for her, where to find the paperwork, and how to reach his lawyer if she needed anything. She nodded and said she understood, but she was barely listening. She was barely able to absorb anything past the fact that the man she loved was gone again—and this time, he might never be coming back.

"Goodbye, Simone," he said, his voice full of emotion. "I love you."

"I love you, too." She waited for him to say more, to keep her on the phone and turn around and come back home. Instead, the line turned silent.

Simone swallowed, hanging up the phone and pushing it back into her pocket. She asked the taxi driver to take her back to Teagan's apartment, then leaned back against the dull black seat and closed her eyes. Tears slipped down her cheeks, but she held her breath, keeping the sobbing at bay.

Everything was ruined. And it was all that woman's fault.

A new conviction ran through her at the thought of Serena Mercer. Grant had said that there was nothing she could do, but she refused to believe that. She refused to sit on the sidelines and wait for life to run her over, then back over her again.

She was tired of being a victim. Tired of being the person who helped everyone else, but in this situation, she had to do it once more. She was going to fight to bring Grant back home, back into her life. She was going to be the person who helped others—but this time, it wasn't just for Grant.

It was for her.

CHAPTER TWENTY-SEVEN

GRANT HAD BEEN in prison for two months. That was sixty days that he had been behind bars. The thought made Simone sick to her stomach. She swirled the wine around in her glass at the hotel bar where she was sitting then downed the rest in a few quick gulps.

Standing, she smoothed out her skirt and then made her way around the bar to the far end. She slid into the bar seat next to a statuesque redhead. "Serena."

Serena swirled on her barstool to face her. Her eyes widened for only a second, then showed just the tiniest hint of recognition before she lifted her chin and tensed her jaw, as if steeling herself for the confrontation. "I don't think I ever got your name," she replied.

Simone stretched out a hand. "Simone Reynolds."

The beautiful redhead glanced down at Simone's hand, but didn't take it. "I would say it's nice to officially meet you, but something tells me this isn't just a social call."

"He broke up with me, you know." Her words came out slightly slurred, that third glass of wine beginning to slow her reflexes. She tilted forward to lean on the bar but missed. Her arms slid down to her lap instead. Simone righted herself, then pointed at Serena. "He broke up with me because of you."

A sly smile spread across the woman's face. "You're drunk. Maybe you should run on home and stop embarrassing yourself."

Simone shook her head, her finger still wagging in front of the woman's face. "No. You don't get to talk. I get to talk. You ruined everything. It's your fault he's in jail."

"I don't know what my good-for-nothing ex-husband told you," Serena replied, her voice lowered as she leaned forward. "But his lot in life is his own fault."

"I loved him, Serena." Simone picked up Serena's wine glass and downed the entire thing. "I loved him and you ruined it."

Serena glanced around them, clearly annoyed by her display. "Can you *please* lower your voice?"

"Can I?" Simone's voice only rose louder. "CAN I LOWER MY VOICE?"

"Jesus Christ." Serena slid off her barstool and grabbed Simone's elbow, yanking her alongside her and guiding her to the bathroom at the end of a long hallway off the bar.

"Hey!" Simone protested, but let the woman drag her along anyway. "Ow!"

"I can't even believe Grant would go from being married to someone like me to dating a complete mess like you," Serena huffed. "What a joke."

"Hey," Simone protested again, less conviction in her voice this time.

"How did you even find me?" Serena asked, wetting some paper towel in the sink and holding it to Simone's forehead in a sad attempt at sobering her up. "No one's been able to find me."

"I just saw you here." Simone's words stumbled out of her mouth. "I was drinking."

"No shit." Serena shook her head, crossing her arms over her chest. "You smell like the inside of a wine bottle."

"Hey!"

Serena leaned closer. "Listen, I'm sorry, okay? Is that what you want to hear? Will that make you leave me alone?"

"Why did you do it?" Simone asked, coughing at the last word. "Why did you frame him for stealing all that money?"

Serena shrugged. "It wasn't that hard. I fell in love, and we needed money to run off together. I wasn't about to take the heat myself. I already knew Grant's passwords. It was so easy to take every dime."

"But you didn't even care? You didn't care about ruining his life?" Tears sprung to Simone's eyes at the thought.

"Why should I care about a man who never cared about me?" Serena checked her reflection in the mirror, running her fingers through her hair. "Grant worked all the time. He was barely ever home, and when he was...I don't know. We just didn't have that spark. Not like I've felt with other men."

"Then why get married in the first place?"

"That's easy," Serena replied, the sly smile returning to her face again. "He was going places in his career. He was always going to be rich. Why not share the wealth?"

"Are you saying you married him for his money, and then stole all of it? Even framed him for embezzlement?" Simone repeated back the story, wanting to be clear on the exact story.

Serena let out a loud sigh. "Yes, yes, yes. Okay? Are you happy now to know the truth? Will that help you forgive him? I'm doing you a favor by telling you this. Maybe I'm a romantic at heart and want you two crazy kids to work out."

She shook her head again, laughing to herself. "Of course I married him for his wealth. Of course I stole the money and framed him. It's not that hard of a concept. Maybe if you weren't so drunk, you'd get that through your thick head."

Simone straightened up, pulling the cell phone out of her front pocket. She showed the screen to Serena, an image of a microphone showing that she had been recording the entire conversation. With a few quick clicks, the recording from their conversation was being sent to Grant's lawyer immediately. The moment she confirmed it had been sent, Simone lifted her gaze back up to Serena, smiling widely.

"What...what was that?" Serena asked, panic beginning to light in her eyes.

Simone tossed her hair over her shoulder. "I'm actually not drunk at all, though I did practically bathe in whiskey so I'd smell like it. Grant's investigators found out where you've been staying, and they agreed to let me come and try to get the confession from you. Turns out, you talk pretty easily."

Serena stepped closer to her. "I don't know what you think you've got on me—"

"You mean an entire confession to being a thief and a horrible wife?" Simone slid her phone back in her pocket. "I think I've got enough. It was nice seeing you again, Serena. I hope you don't plan on returning to New Zealand anytime soon. And if you don't return, I hope you enjoy a life always looking over your shoulder for the minute that they're going to get you, because, Serena? They will get you."

"You fucking bitch," Serena shouted, reaching her hand forward to slap her.

Simone jumped out of the way just in time, then waved and headed for the bathroom exit. "Enjoy your freedom while it lasts, Serena. I'm going to go get my man out of prison."

She walked out, hearing the string of curses coming from Serena behind her. Her phone began to ring, and she quickly answered it.

"Hello?"

"Simone, it's Andrew. That was brilliant."

Simone smiled at the compliment from Grant's lawyer. "Will it help?"

"That combined with her current financials, showing she has the money and is currently living off the remainder of it? I'm certain they'll let him go," Andrew told her. "It's not going to be overnight, though. It'll be a few days at best, but probably longer."

She groaned, frustrated that the legal system was always so difficult, no matter where one lived. "I just need him home soon, Andrew. I need him home."

"I understand. This is my top priority until I put him on the plane back to the States. You have my word." With that, he hung up and Simone headed out of the hotel bar and onto the sidewalk.

Soon.

CHAPTER TWENTY-EIGHT

GRANT STRETCHED HIS NECK, moving his head from one side to the other. The cramped airplane seat was causing every muscle in his giant frame to ache, but he wasn't about to complain. Hell, this was the most comfortable he'd been in months. Spending the last sixty-plus days behind bars had been one of the worst experiences of his entire life in so many ways.

The entire situation had been professionally humiliating, causing him to have to postpone his new assignment on a film set in Vancouver due to his predicament. That had been an uncomfortable conversation to have with his superiors. Thankfully, they'd agreed to use another composer in the interim and then bring him back on the project if, or when, he was released. He'd be heading up there shortly to complete the end of the assignment after he spent some time at home in New York City.

But his career or any of that never really mattered to him, not as much as losing Simone had hit him. Lying to her about his past was something he was never going to do again —or just lying in general. If she'd give him the opportunity to make it up to him, to give him a second chance, he was going to do everything in his power to prove to her that she was everything to him. She came before work, before anything. Sure, his job often took him away from home, and that was something that had hurt his previous relationship, but he knew that he and Simone could make it work. If they couldn't, then he'd quit. He'd do whatever he had to do to keep her.

After convincing her to take him back.

The airplane's wheels finally hit the tarmac, and they taxied to the gate. He quickly disembarked, swinging him carry-on over his shoulder. The sooner he got in a cab and to their penthouse, the sooner he'd be able to see Simone.

"Grant!" A familiar voice called out to him as he left through the exit and into baggage claim.

He spotted Simone standing near the exit, their fluffy little dog in her arms. His heart nearly leaped out of his chest at the sight of her. By her side in seconds, he gathered her into his arms.

"What are you doing here?" he asked, burying his face in her hair. "Oh, God, I've missed you."

"Andrew gave me your flight information," she replied, wrapping one arm around his neck while her over hand held their dog sandwiched between them. "I couldn't wait to see you."

He held her at arm's length for a moment, just taking her in. Her skin was slightly darker with a summer tan, her tattoos even darker. There was a tinge of blue at the ends of her wavy locks now, barely visible and yet very her. Her dark brown eyes were the same, full of life and lined with tears threatening to well over.

His hands moved to her face, holding her. "I had a whole speech I was going to rehearse, and I was going to buy flowers. I want you to trust me again, to see that I'm not the man I was before. I won't make those mistakes again—I'll *never* lie to you again. I love you, Simone, and I'll do anything to convince you to give me a second chance."

She shook her head, a few tears sliding down her cheek that he wiped away with his thumbs. "I don't need a speech, and I don't need convincing. I've already forgiven you. I love you, Grant."

He swallowed hard, his heart pumping harder in his chest. "Fuck, Simone...that's the best thing I've ever heard."

Leaning down, he placed his lips to hers. Soft, gentle, and everything he'd been dreaming about for the last two months while lying on a hard, metal cot in a shitty jail cell with no windows. Every moment of that hell seemed worth it now. To have her in his arms, nothing chasing him, nothing hidden.

Completely free.

"Come on," she whispered against his lips. "Let's go home."

"That sounds perfect," he admitted, then took Millie into his arms and lifted her to his face. He let her lick his cheek, laughing and then burying his face in her fur. "I missed you, too, pup." He turned to Simone. "She's so much bigger than I remember."

She nodded. "Puppies grow fast."

Grant tucked the dog under his arm and then took Simone's hand as they walked toward the curb and flagged down a cab. Within thirty minutes, they were pulling up in front of their building and heading into the lobby, and a few minutes after that, they were walking into the apartment.

"Holy crap..." Grant's eyes went wide as he looked around their home. Last time he'd seen it, they'd had a bed and a chair, and that was about it. But now, the place was completely furnished and beautifully decorated. It was like looking at a home decorating magazine, that was how perfect everything was. "Simone, this is amazing."

She placed Millie down on the carpet. "It's a little different than when you saw it last," she kidded.

"Definitely," he replied, a slight chuckle under his words. "You've done an amazing job. I'm so impressed."

"All of your things are here, too. I set up your closet and drawers and kept everything untouched until you got home." Her words slightly choked up on the end. "I just knew you were going to come home."

He took her in his arms, pinning her against his chest. "I'm just happy you wanted me to come home. I can't even begin to thank you for everything you did to help my release. Tricking Serena? I'm so sorry you even had to be so involved in my mess, but, damn, I'm so happy you did that."

"It was actually pretty fun," Simone admitted, laughing. Her smile lit up her entire face, and his heart pumped faster at the very sight of it. Seeing her happy and smiling? That's all he ever wanted from here on out. "I might be a singer at heart, but I think I've got this acting thing down."

"You are very talented," he agreed, thinking of having seen her acting in *Kiss Me, Kate*. "I wish I could have seen the look on her face when she realized you'd duped her."

Simone bit her bottom lip, trying to keep from smiling too wide. He loved that she was trying not to enjoy it too much, even though she clearly was.

"It was priceless. I wish I had snapped a picture, but I was too busy sending the recording to Andrew."

Grant nodded, still grateful to his lawyer and friend for doing so much work to get him released. He had no doubt that if it wasn't for Andrew and Simone, he'd probably have been convicted and spending the full ten-year sentence in jail.

"As grateful as I am, I'm still sorry you had to do that," he replied.

"Hey, this is 2018," she teased, running her hands down his arms. "Damsels can save princes now."

Grant laughed, tipping his head backward. "You're anything but a damsel. You're a princess, a goddamn warrior. None of us stood a chance against you."

"Glad you recognize greatness." She gestured to herself, then giggled and shook it off. "Speaking of saving your ass... you owe me."

He lifted one brow. "Is that so?"

"I think you can pay me back in...let's say, the bedroom?" Simone nodded down the hallway. "After all, you've got to have a tour of the *whole* apartment."

"I have been here before, you know," he joked. "I do know where the bedroom is."

She giggled, a naughty tone at the end of her laughter. "Sure, *buuuuut* you haven't tested out the new sheets and comforter I got for the bed. It's so important to really give it a good feel."

The corners of his lips twitched into a smile. "Oh, I definitely want to feel...the sheets." With one quick move, he lunged toward her, but she slipped from his grasp, laughing.

She began to run toward the bedroom, but he was only a few steps behind. Sweeping her up in his arms, he filled up on her laughter and smiles before placing her on the bed and climbing on top of her.

"God, I've missed this," he said with a deep groan.

"You can't even imagine," she replied, her lips brushing against his cheek.

He found her mouth with his, kissing her with a frenzied fervor that months apart had created. Going slow wasn't even on his radar and based on the way her body writhed beneath his, it wasn't on hers either.

Every ounce of him wanted to be buried deep inside her, but he had other priorities first. Gripping her shirt's bottom hem, he slid the garment up over her head and tossed it to the floor, then he unbuttoned her jeans and slid those and her panties down her legs in one quick move, leaving them on the floor as well. She was flush beneath him, her nipples pressing against the lace fabric of her bra and her hips lifting to meet his.

"Grant," she begged, though she didn't even know what he had planned.

Grinning, he dipped his head to her neck, licking slowly across her skin to her collarbone then traveling even lower to her breasts. He pushed the cups of her bra down, taking one nipple between his teeth with a gentle nip before sucking hard.

She groaned beneath him, shivering and clutching his biceps. He loved the way she'd always gripped his arms, as she'd once told him that was one of her favorite body parts on him. To know she was turning herself on touching him... fuck, he loved it almost as much as he loved her.

With a gentle breath against her skin, he moved farther south and pushed her knees apart, crawling in between. She squirmed against him as she realized what he was doing, but he held her still with his large hands against her thighs. When his tongue met her core, she gasped and her body began to tremble. Quick flicks of his tongue against her most sensitive bundle of nerves had her hips bucking against him as she cried out in pleasure.

He growled against her body. "Come for me, Simone."

She quivered as her release began to take over, but his

hands continued to hold her still as his tongue slid across every inch of her until she completely fell apart. When she finally began to quiet, only soft whimpers coming from her as her climax slowly dissipated, he quickly undressed and crawled back up her body until he found her mouth.

They kissed, and he pressed his length against her stomach. He was so hard, he wasn't sure he'd last long, but damn if she didn't make him feel out of control. Seeing every inch of her body, hearing every sound from her lips, it went straight to his dick and made him throb for her.

She pinned her knees to either side of his hips and reached between their bodies, taking his length in her hand and guiding him to her entrance.

"We need a condom," he reminded her, trying to be sensible even in the haze that he was currently under.

She shook her head. "I started the pill."

"You did?" Fuck, that was perfect.

"I want to feel you inside me," she continued. "You're it for me, Grant. I love you."

Grant kissed her hard, growling against her lips as he pushed inside her completely. "I love you, baby. I fucking love you so much."

She giggled, only to be interrupted by a moan as he stretched every inch of her with his width. "Oh, God..."

"You feel amazing," he whispered against her ear, thrusting harder and faster as he enjoyed every sensation of her body pulsing and clenching around him. "For the rest of my life, Simone...this is mine. You're mine."

She nodded, panting. "Yes, please."

He continued to pump in and out of her until he was barely seconds from exploding. "Come with me, Simone. I want to feel you undone against my dick."

She was already trembling, panting hard as she pressed

her hips against his in rhythm with his thrusts. "I'm so close," she replied, and then she was.

He could feel her climax roaring through her, and it pushed him over the edge he'd been so precariously balancing on. Grunting, he came inside her, clutching her body as close to his as they could possibly be. He wanted to feel every inch of her, and never be parted again. If he could live the rest of his life skin-to-skin with her, he would.

"Holy shit," he said with a groan as he fell onto the bed next to her once they had both calmed down. "That was incredible."

She nodded, still trying to catch her breath. "Amazing."

"Maybe I should go to jail more often."

Simone laughed then smacked him on the chest. "Don't you dare."

He grinned, pushing up on one elbow to lean over and look at her. "I'm never leaving you again, Simone."

Her eyes glistened as she stared back at him. "Promise?"

He nodded slowly, because if there was one promise he could make in this world, it was that. He would never let them be apart like that again. Sure, he'd have to leave for work, but he'd come back every weekend to visit, or fly her out to see him. He'd call every day. He'd make the effort that he'd never made in his marriage.

She was it for him, and he was never letting go.

"I promise," he replied so softly, it was almost a whisper. "I belong here. I belong with you."

Her fingers gently brushed his cheek, then she cupped his face. "I trust you."

Leaning down, he kissed her once, then twice. Then forever more.

EPILOGUE

A YEAR LATER

"This is a *big* step," Simone said, glancing nervously over at Grant from the passenger seat of the car as they drove through New Zealand's countryside.

Grant slid his hand around the wheel, steering them closer to his family's home. "My parents are going to love you, babe. Plus, we've been living together for almost a year. The fact that you've only met them via video chat is insane."

"I know. I know." She sighed, fussing with the edge of her shirt, readjusting it for the fifteenth time. "I just really want them to like me. After all, it's my fault you don't live here anymore. They can't be thrilled that I'm the woman who made you move to New York."

Grant chuckled, pushing his hair behind his ear. "Simone, you didn't *make* me move anywhere. My job brings me to New York a lot, and I would never want to live somewhere you're not."

He could see her chewing her bottom lip out of the corner of his eye. "Maybe we should have invited them to New York sooner. They can come stay with us for a few weeks this winter or something?"

"Actually, my mother was mentioning coming to the States for Christmas," Grant admitted.

She perked up, leaning across the console to squeeze his leg. "See? Perfect! They won't be mad once they see how awesome our life out there is. Or when they meet Millie!"

"They aren't mad now," Grant reassured her again. "But, man, now I miss Millie."

Simone frowned. "I know. At least she's bonded with our neighbor. Nice of them to dog-sit for us."

Grant nodded, agreeing. He'd keep her talking as long as possible as long as the subject stayed off of what he had planned when they arrived at his parents' house. He'd been organizing this surprise for months, and it had taken a shit ton of coordination to make all the pieces fall into place.

"Do you think I'm dressed okay?" Simone asked, although she'd already asked twice—once at the airport, and once at the beginning of the ride in their rental car.

He reached over and took her hand, giving her a small squeeze. "Babe, relax. Take a deep breath or something. You look gorgeous. My parents are going to love you. It's going to be an amazing trip and everything is absolutely fine."

She grinned, intertwining her fingers with his. "Am I annoying you? All my worrying?"

"Not at all. I just don't like seeing you stressed."

"Is it weird I just feel like there's something I'm missing?" Simone tapped a finger against her chin. "I just feel like I've overlooked something."

Grant bit his lip, hoping she was still none the wiser to his plan. "Now you're just looking for things to stress about."

"You're right." She sighed. "God, this drive is gorgeous. I can't even believe you used to live here. I don't know if I'd give up this view for a smoggy city full of high rises."

"I still have my house here," he reminded her. "We can

come stay here during the summers or breaks from work. What about when you're done with this season of *Imagine?*"

Simone had been cast in an hour-long musical drama that had quickly become a huge hit across the country. The show focused on a group of Broadway stars and their life outside of the show, and she was quickly eclipsing the rest of the cast with her incredible acting skills and even better singing voice.

He was so proud of her for all her successes, and he couldn't quite figure out how she did it all. While filming the show, she had also recorded her first solo album that was set to launch next month. He'd witnessed her blood, sweat, and tears go into the record, and it was definitely some of the best he'd ever heard from her. She'd even finished her joint project with Lily Allen and it had been every bit the success that the record label producers had suspected it would be.

"Won't you still be working on the *Legends* soundtrack?" she asked, rubbing her thumb across the back of his hand. The smallest act, and yet his heart filled with love at every-thing she did.

Grant had been hired to do the soundtrack to a mixed martial arts fighter movie chronicling the rise and fall of a famous fighter from the Bronx. It was some of the most grip-ping work he'd ever done, capturing the grittiness and edgi-ness of the script into the musical score. He'd had a chance to meet the fighter it was based on, Rory Kavanagh, and gotten all the inspiration he'd needed to pound out the perfect composition.

"I'll be done around the same time, give or take a few days."

"Really?" Simone turned to him, her face breaking into a smile. "Are you saying we might actually get a vacation?"

Grant wiggled his brows. "I think we will."

"Let's do it." Simone let go of his hand and then clapped her hands together. "We have worked so hard this last year. We need it."

"I agree," Grant replied, already looking forward to getting some downtime. He pointed to a large house on top of a hill in front of them. "Here's my parents' house."

Simone gasped. "Oh, it's *gorgeous*, Grant. Absolutely breathtaking."

After he'd reached some success, he'd built the house for his parents to retire in. It was their dream home, and he had felt so honored he'd been able to give back to them in such a way. They'd always been there to support him his entire life, and it meant so much to him to be able to repay their many, many favors.

"Thanks." He pulled the car up the drive and parked to the side. Opening his door, he climbed out and rounded the car before opening Simone's door and escorting her out.

She smiled at him, taking his hand. "Such a gentleman."

"Outside of the bedroom," he teased, earning a light smack on the chest from Simone.

"You're impossible."

Grant chuckled, leading her up the stairs to the front door. Anticipation built inside him as he thought of what was to come. His hand felt his front pocket, triple checking that the small, square box was still there.

The front door swung open and his mother stood in the doorway. She looked exactly like he remembered from the last time he'd seen her in person when she'd visited him in prison, though there were more lines around her mouth and eyes and her hair was almost entirely gray now.

"Grant!" She reached her arms out to him. "I've been watching for you! I'm so happy to see you." They embraced and she squeezed him tightly before letting go and turning to Simone. "You must be Simone."

"I am," Simone confirmed, reaching out a hand. "It's lovely to meet you, Mrs. Mercer."

His mother pushed Simone's hand to the side. "We're huggers in this family, darling. And call me Maggie."

Grant grinned at the blush on Simone's cheeks as she hugged his mother. His father quickly showed up in the front entryway as well—tall and statuesque with a permanent smile stuck to his face. Grant wasn't sure he'd ever seen his father not looking happy. The man just oozed contentment.

"Grant!" His father pulled him in for a hug as well. "Good to see you, son. Is this your lovely girl?"

Simone had finished hugging his mother, turning to her father next. She didn't even bother reaching out a hand this time and just went straight for the hug. "I'm Simone. It's wonderful to meet you."

"Call me Mark, sweetheart," he replied.

Simone lifted a brow to Grant. "Maggie and Mark Mercer? But named you Grant?"

Grant chuckled, shrugging. "I don't have any more answers than you do."

"Come in, come in." Mark gestured toward the foyer, ushering them inside. "We've got some guests here you might recognize."

"Guests?" Simone looked confused but followed them inside.

Grant hung back, closing the door behind them. He reached his hand inside his pocket, fingering the velvet box.

"Mom?" Simone suddenly squeaked out, coming to a dead stop at the entry to the living room. "Teagan? Aria? Ben? Reed? What the heck? What is going on?"

Simone's entire family, including her nieces and brand-new nephew were all standing in the living room grinning at her.

Simone whirled around to face Grant, but he had already dropped to one knee. "Grant?"

Grant opened the velvet box in his hand, revealing a large, sparkling diamond ring. "Simone, I know how much your family means to you, probably because my family means so much to me, too. So, I realized that the best way to ask you to be a part of my life forever would be to involve everyone we love. I flew your entire family here because I love them just as much as I love you. I don't just want to marry you, Simone. I want to combine our entire lives—our families, our futures. I want to walk side-by-side with you for the rest of my life." He took a deep breath, trying not to be too distracted by the tears in her eyes or the way she trembled as she looked down at him. "Simone Marie Reynolds, will you marry me?"

Simone wiped at her eyes, her head nodding. "Of course. Of course I'll marry you."

Grant grinned, getting to his feet and taking her hand in his. He slid the ring onto her finger as tears streamed down both of their faces. "I'm so fucking happy," he told her, leaning down and placing a kiss against her lips.

She tried to speak, but nothing came out, her tears still getting the better of her.

Aria was the first to give them a giant hug. "Congratulations, guys."

"Thank you," Simone finally managed to say as everyone in both of their families took turns hugging them both and congratulating them on their engagement.

"All right, time to eat!" his mother announced, showing everyone to the large dining room in front of a giant glass wall that overlooked the expansive yard and landscaping. "I cooked enough for a feast!"

Grant hung back, his arms still wrapped around Simone.

"Babe, I had no idea," she murmured against his cheek as she kissed down the line of his jaw. "I can't believe you organized all of this and I had no clue."

He chuckled, touching his lips to hers. "I've still got a few tricks up my sleeves."

"You never cease to amaze me," she teased, taking his face in her hands and kissing him harder. They pressed their lips together tightly, as if they couldn't get enough. He didn't want enough. He wanted everything. He wanted her.

Grant vowed then and there to do everything he could to make Simone feel loved and cherished every day for the rest of their lives together. He was never going to allow his life to go off the rails like it had done once before. This time, he was getting it right.

Because this time, she was just right.

SERIES EPILOGUE

*T*HIS SHORT EPILOGUE *revisits all of the Reynolds' sisters and their partners five years in the future and is the final appearance of the Reynolds family.*

Aria

"I FEEL like I'm more nervous about today than I was for my own wedding," Aria said, turning to look at her mother where she was seated on a long chaise lounge in Aria's bedroom. Aria stood in front of the floor length mirror next to the window, overlooking the festivities in their backyard.

"Why?" Betty Reynolds replied. "You're already married. A vow renewal is basically just a sentimental party."

Aria chuckled, amused by the fact that her mother had never really gotten on board with the concept of her marrying Ben...again. But it was the ten-year anniversary since their first wedding, and they had wanted to celebrate that milestone with their children and family.

"Mom!" Tyson, Aria's three-year-old son, came barreling into the room with his two older sisters on his heels.

He looked just like his father, and Aria loved seeing Ben's bright blue eyes on their little boy. True looked like Aria's miniature twin and was five years old now, while her older sister, Tillie, was almost nine years old and looked like the perfect cross between Ben and Aria.

Tyson threw his arms around her legs. "Mom! Mom! Guess what!"

"Baby, careful!" Aria chided, trying to keep her off-white lace dress from being ruined by sticky fingers. "What happened to the corn hole game you all were playing outside?"

"It's throwing bags in a hole, Mom," Tillie said, all the attitude of a teenage even though she was still years away. She perched one hand on her hip and tilted her head. "It's for babies."

Aria laughed. "A lot of adults play corn hole, you know. Especially when they're drinking."

"Drinking what?" True piped up. "Can I have a drink? You said we could have a soda today!"

"One soda," Aria reminded them. She tried to be as healthy as possible with her children's diets, but today was a special day and she was definitely going to let them splurge.

"All right, all right," Aria's mother interrupted, ushering the children toward the door. "Your mother has to finish getting dressed for the ceremony. Go downstairs and find your Auntie Teagan and sit with her. We're getting started soon."

"And then soda?" True asked.

Betty laughed. "And then all the soda you want."

"One soda," Aria added, because if she let her, Betty would run wild with spoiling her grandkids.

Betty ushered the children outside into the hallway, then returned to Aria's side in the mirror. Her mother was wearing a light blue two-piece skirt and blazer and looked beautifully matronly. Aria was sad that her father wasn't going to be here, but he had been at her first wedding, which was certainly a blessing. Her youngest sister, Simone, hadn't had that joy, and it had definitely been a painful moment for her on her wedding day to Grant.

"You look gorgeous," Betty said, smiling at her in their reflection. "Ben's a lucky man."

"Ten years, Ma." Aria shook her head, still barely able to wrap her mind around everywhere her life had gone in the last dozen years since she'd met Ben. "I can't believe how much has changed."

"I always knew you were destined for big things, baby girl," Betty murmured, a slight nostalgia tinting her tone. "But, man, even I couldn't have guessed what the last few years would hold."

Aria had received her third Academy Award last year, this time for playing a cancer patient who chose to end her own life in a major motion picture that had ended up winning a slew of awards, not just for Best Actress. Her non-profit that supported women's rights in Hollywood and around the globe had turned into a multi-million-dollar empire that gave back all of its profits to women in need. She'd won dozens of humanitarian awards, and earlier this year, they'd built their first school exclusively for little girls in Africa. Aria had overseen the entire project, spending quite a bit of time out there making sure their vision was executed correctly.

But as much as she'd grown and flourished over the last

decade, they'd had their hardships as well. Despite the fact that they'd had three beautiful children, she and Ben had lost two pregnancies in between, and it had nearly broken her heart. Her father had passed away, as well as Ben's best friend, and agent, Arthur Atwood, who'd been like a father to him after losing his own father at a young age. They'd faced multiple tabloid scandals, most completely fabricated, and she'd hit a rocky patch in her marriage last year when all of those things seemed to happen at one time. Ben had actually gone to stay in a hotel for a few weeks, and Aria was sure her entire world was collapsing around her. And yet, with a little counseling and a lot of love and dedication, they had kept their marriage together through those rocky heartbreaks.

That was one of the reasons why today was so important to her. They'd worked hard to hit this ten-year milestone, and she wasn't going to take it for granted. She knew without a doubt now how difficult making a long-term marriage last could be. She was going to celebrate their success, because that's exactly what it was. Even with all the hardships, there was one thing that they never lost or let go of, and that was love. She loved Ben with her whole heart. He was her person, her other half, her everything, and she knew without a shadow of a doubt that she was his.

There was a soft knock on the door, and both women turned to see Ben sticking his head in.

A smile spread across Aria's face. "Hey."

"Hey, beautiful," he replied, smiling as well. "Betty, would you mind if I have a moment alone with my gorgeous wife?"

Betty nodded. "Okay, but the ceremony is supposed to start any minute, so don't waste any more time." She headed out the door, closing it behind her and leaving them alone.

"You're supposed to be down at the end of the aisle waiting for me," Aria teased, running her hand down the lapel of his suit. God, he looked amazing in a suit and even though he was older, small lines around his eyes and white hair on the edges of his temples, she was still as attracted to him today as she'd been the first time she met him.

He wrapped his arms around her waist and pulled her flush against his body. "I couldn't wait. I just needed to hold you."

She could feel her cheeks heating, a blush creeping over her face. The fact that he still made her giddy, still made her stomach flip-flop with butterflies all these years later...

"I can't believe it's been ten years," he murmured against her skin as he buried his face in her neck. "I love you, Aria. I love the way you still make me feel—lovesick and impulsive with need. I love the way you mother our children, the way you shower them with love and attention despite how busy our lives can be. I love the career woman you've turned into, and how you've never once let all your success go to your head. When you walk down the aisle to me today, I won't just be remarrying the young woman I met twelve years ago. I won't just be reaffirming that decision we made ten years ago to marry. I'll be remarrying the woman you are now, the woman I've decided to love every day for the last decade, the woman who has made me the man I am today. I couldn't live without you, Aria, and I would never want to."

Her heart swelled in her chest, an overwhelming feeling of affection and love bubbling up inside her as she wrapped her arms around his neck. "I love you, Ben. You're my whole life. You always will be."

He kissed her, hard and full of passion, a teaser of what was to come when they were alone again.

Ben growled, and she could feel the rumble in his chest.

"Let's make everyone wait a little longer..." His hand slid up her leg, sliding underneath her dress.

Aria giggled but pushed him away. "I don't think so, mister. You're going to mess up my dress."

"Might be worth it," he teased, placing kisses across her shoulder and then grabbing her waist and lifting her on to the edge of the windowsill. She didn't even care if people below could see them, though they were so high up that she doubted they could.

He slid her dress up her legs, his fingers brushing in between. She was already ready—hell, she always was when he was around. Time had done nothing to change her body's reaction to him. From the bulge pressing against the front of his suit pants, she could tell that he felt the exact same way.

She moaned, her head falling back against the glass pane. "Oh, God..."

"Is that a yes?" He kissed her again, their tongues dancing as she gripped his lapels to keep him flush against her.

"Please..." She was begging now, spreading her legs as he pushed her panties aside and unbuttoned his pants.

He positioned himself in between her legs, pressing at her entrance and then plunging inside. She held on to him as he thrust inside her at a frenzied rhythm as her climax already began building inside her.

"I'm close," he said with a groan, his fingers gripping her hips tightly.

She panted, trying to catch her breath but quickly getting lost in her own release as it began to tip over the edge and send her spiraling down. "Oh, Ben!" She gasped as it finally hit her, and he pumped harder, reaching his own release at the same time.

They breathed hard together, their foreheads against one another as they tried to come down from the moment. Finally, he stepped back and fixed himself back into his pants as she readjusted her dress.

Ben lifted one brow, staring at her with a small half-smile.

"What?" she asked. "What's the smile for?"

His small smile widened into a wicked grin. "I love the idea of you walking down the aisle with my cum inside you."

She smacked his chest lightly. "You are such a perv."

"Only for you," he teased, giving her a wink and then kissing her. "I'll see you in a few minutes downstairs. I'll be the lucky bastard at the end of the aisle."

She kissed him back. "I love you."

"I love you more," he said before leaving.

Aria turned back to look at her reflection in the mirror, fixing her hair and makeup to try and make the last fifteen minutes not look as obvious. She was more than ready to walk down that aisle and pledge the next ten-years, and the rest of her life, to the man she loved.

Despite every role she played in her life, her favorite had always been, and would always be, Mrs. Ben Lawson.

Teagan

"DID THEY CALL YOU YET?" Teagan whispered to Reed where they were sitting in the second row at Aria and Ben's vow renewal. It hadn't started yet—in fact, it was running a few minutes behind.

Reed shook his head, bouncing their son, Porter, on his

knee in an attempt to keep him distracted while they waited. Porter was still pretty small for his age and strangely enough, looked exactly like the young version of Teagan's father. Their daughter, Piper, was seated next to them, staying perfectly quiet since she was playing on an iPad with headphones. Technology was the best babysitter.

"They haven't called yet, but I put my phone on silent for the ceremony," he told her.

"Can't you just put it on vibrate?" she asked. "I really don't want to miss their call. This could be it—today could be the day!"

He chuckled and leaned over to kiss her on the cheek. "Babe, even if we do get the call, it's not going to be today. We'd have to travel to wherever the child is, wait for the delivery, then it'll be several days or weeks before we can take the baby home."

She knew he was right, but this entire process had been so exhausting and exhilarating all at once. After having two children, they'd decided not to have any more of their own. Being pregnant was a huge roadblock to her career as a dancer, but even then, they both knew that they'd always wanted to give a home to a child in need.

A few weeks ago, they'd finally been paired with a young, teenage mother who was giving up the rights to her child. The road was going to be difficult, because their future child was going to be born with a cocaine dependency. There was no doubt that it would be an uphill battle to bring this baby to full health, and every ounce of Teagan was terrified that their future baby wouldn't make it.

Her due date was next month, so now they were just waiting for the call that it was time. The doctor had warned them that it was likely the mother would deliver early because of the drug use during the pregnancy and other complications from the baby's lack of nutrition. So, they were prepared. Everything was already ready—the nursery, the tiny baby clothes, the formula. But even being fully ready, she couldn't help her nerves at the entire process.

If the baby arrived and didn't make it, Teagan was certain her heart would completely break. She'd been to the ultrasounds, she'd met the mother, she'd spoken to her future baby. She was already in love with him, and they'd already named him Pace.

He already felt like theirs.

"Don't worry," Reed reassured her, wrapping one arm around her shoulders. "This baby is going to come, and when he does, he'll be okay. We've prayed so much for him. He's going to be okay."

Teagan leaned against her husband's shoulder, sighing and hoping that he was right. Something about the way he spoke to her, the way he just seemed to *know* it was all going to be all right...she believed him. She'd always believed him.

Their family was at the core of who they were, the core of their entire lives. Teagan had found that her true love was in Broadway, so while she still did the occasional dance film, including being on *Break Down 4* now, she continued to work on the stage. She'd won several awards for her work, and while that wasn't why she did it, she loved the recognition for all her hard work.

Reed had continued acting, starring in film after film that continued to be box office successes. He mostly worked in romantic comedies and had gained quite a name for himself in that field. Paparazzi continued to follow him around, but Teagan didn't even mind anymore. He was great at what he did, and he loved doing it.

The best part about his work is that the filming wasn't

long, and often he was able to take jobs in New York City where they lived or taken them to the set with him. Their family was rarely apart if they could help it, and even when they were, he'd come home every free moment he had. Being a father and husband was Reed's number one priority, and Teagan felt that love and dedication from him every day.

"I love you," she whispered, placing a quick kiss on his cheek.

He smiled at her, those light green eyes sparkling every time he looked at her. "I love you, too." Suddenly his eyes widened. "Oh, shit."

"What?"

"My pocket just vibrated." He reached down and fished out his phone.

"Oh my God, is it time?" Teagan leaned over to see the screen. Sure enough, it was their lawyer. "Holy shit!"

"Hello?" Reed answered the phone quietly, and Teagan leaned in to listen to the conversation.

"Mr. Scott, how are you doing?" the lawyer said.

"Great," Reed replied. "What's going on?"

"It looks like we might have a baby soon!" he explained, excitement in his voice. "She's at the hospital, but the contractions are very far apart. The doctor said it's still going to be quite a wait, but everything looks like it's going well so far."

"Isn't it too early?" Reed asked, clutching the phone tighter.

"It's early," the lawyer agreed. "So, the baby will probably be kept at the hospital for some time, especially with his complications already. But I'll go ahead and text you the room information, so come on down when you can. It's almost time for you to meet your son."

Reed reached over and squeezed Teagan's hand. "Thank you. We'll be there as soon as possible." Then he hung up the phone.

"It's time," Teagan whispered, her eyes widening. "We have to go!"

"Go tell your sister," he said, already beginning to stand up. "I'll get the kids in the car."

"Reed?" she paused for a moment, her hand on his forearm. "I love you."

He grinned. "I love you, baby. You're the best mom to these two I could ever have dreamed of. I know you're going to be just as amazing with Pace."

Teagan grinned, placing a soft kiss on her husband's lips. "You're the best thing that's ever happened to me."

"Right back at you, beautiful."

SIMONE

THERE WAS ABSOLUTELY NOTHING MORE uncomfortable than being on stage singing to a small crowd of people waiting for a vow renewal to start while also being nine months pregnant and feeling like a bloated whale.

Simone ran her hand over her giant belly, continuing to croon into the microphone. Honestly, she had agreed to sing at her older sister's vow renewal as a favor, but definitely hadn't expected it to last this long. She wondered what was delaying them.

Grant was sitting in the front row, and he blew her a quick kiss.

Finally, she saw Ben walking up the aisle toward them.

Strangely, Teagan and Reed were also standing up where they were sitting and looked like they were about to leave.

A warm sensation washed over her, and suddenly Simone's eyes widened. *Holy shit, did I just pee myself?* If she was being honest, peeing on herself wasn't entirely a new concept during this pregnancy. She and Grant had only been married for a few months when they'd discovered they were pregnant with their first child, and it had been a huge adjustment for both of them—although they were both thrilled with the news. They'd taken their time getting married and so they certainly hadn't planned on rushing into parenthood, but life had other plans for them.

Grant had moved his parents to New York City in their own apartment so that they would be around for when the baby came. His career had finally steadied out because he'd created and produced a musical on Broadway that was turning into one of the biggest hits New York had seen in decades. The job kept him around, and she was thrilled to have him at home all the time.

Her own career was flourishing with the success of her first solo album, hitting platinum records and earning her a Grammy in the process. It still felt surreal, and she honestly couldn't believe this was her life. She was set to do a tour across the country and internationally about six months after the baby was born, which made her really nervous, but Grant and the baby were going to come with her the entire time.

Still, as famous as she might be now, she had just peed herself in front of a crowd of people. Glancing down between her legs, she realized that there was a giant puddle of liquid around her feet and the bottom of her dress was soaked.

Grant was suddenly standing in front of her. "Babe!"

"Oh my God, hide me," she whispered, trying to hide her mortification. "I peed myself!"

Her husband laughed, gripping her hands. "I think your water just broke, Simone. That's not pee."

She looked down again, then a sudden crack of pain split through her body and she squeezed Grant's hand as a scream rippled through her. "Oh my, God! Was that a contraction? Holy fuck, they're horrible. Oh my, God! The baby is coming! This baby is going to come out of my body! How? Holy shit, I need drugs."

"Simmy?" Teagan was standing next to Grant now. "Are you okay?"

"I need to go to the hospital!" she said, panicking and realizing that a watermelon sized child was about to squeeze through her vagina. Sure, she'd watched the birthing videos, but now that it was about to happen, she was just fucking terrified.

"We're headed there now! Our birth mom is in labor," Teagan replied. "Come on."

She took one of Simone's arms while Grant took the other.

"Let's go!" Ben was by them. "I'll drive!"

"What about the vow renewal?" Simone asked, feeling terrible that she was blocking their plans. "Aria's been so looking forward to today."

"We can always postpone it," Ben replied. "Aria would much rather be here with you. I'll go pull the car around. Reed, go get Aria!"

Twenty minutes later, the entire Reynold's family was at Cedars-Sinai Hospital as Simone was rushed into the delivery room with Grant by her side and everyone else waited in the family area. It was by far one of the most difficult experiences in her entire life, but many, *many* hours later, Simone held their little girl, Mia, in her arms.

"She's as beautiful as you," Grant murmured, gently caressing his daughter's head as he leaned over them. He kissed Simone's head. "You did amazing, babe."

Simone smiled down at Mia. "She's absolutely perfect."

The door to the hospital room pushed open, and Simone's mother stuck her head in. "Is it time to show off my new granddaughter yet?"

Simone nodded, chuckling. "Let them in."

"I'll give you and your sisters a moment," Grant said. He gave her a quick kiss and then left the hospital room.

Betty slipped into his place by Simone's side, oohing and aahing over the baby. Aria was the first to enter, still wearing her lacy vow renewal gown.

"Oh, Aria, I'm so sorry I ruined your big day," Simone said to her older sister.

Aria shook it off. "Don't worry about it, honey. I'm much happier getting to meet my new niece—healthy and beautiful! We rescheduled the vow renewal for next weekend. Already been together ten years, what's one more week?"

"I'm definitely going to be there this time, with a plus one," Simone said, gesturing toward her daughter.

Aria laughed. "She's more than welcome. God, she's gorgeous, Simmy. I can already tell you're going to be an amazing mom."

"Thank you," she replied. And honestly, coming from Aria, one of the best moms she'd ever met, that was a huge compliment. "I'm so in love with her already. Like, I didn't even know this level of love was possible."

Teagan barreled into the room next, her own face aglow with new own news. "Simone! She's gorgeous!" She gazed down at Mia.

"How's Pace?" Simone asked, because she'd been dying to find out the news about her nephew ever since they'd gotten here. "Is he here yet?"

Teagan nodded, her smile lighting up her entire face. Simone immediately recognized that bursting-with-love, new mom expression on Teagan's face. "He's so perfect. He's in the NICU for a while, so I can't bring him to show you, but when you're feeling up to it, we can go see him."

"I can't believe our kids are going to share a birthday," Simone replied, still mesmerized by her own daughter's sleeping face. She couldn't look away, as much as she wanted to give attention to everyone else around her. She could stare at that tiny nose and little lashes all day long.

"Joint birthday parties!" Teagan offered, laughing.

"I think it's good luck," their mother spoke up, gently kissing the head of her new granddaughter. "I know that's what your father would say."

The sisters were quiet for a moment, remembering their late father. Simone wished he'd been here, but she knew he was watching from Heaven.

"I love you ladies," Simone finally said, looking up at her mother and her sisters with tears brimming over her lashes. "I feel so blessed to be part of this family. To be a Reynolds, even if I'm a Mercer now. I feel so honored to be able to bring another woman into our clan. I just...I wouldn't be where I am without you three. I wouldn't be me without you all standing beside me."

Aria swallowed hard, wrapping an arm around Simone's shoulder. "I know what you mean. You all are my world."

Tears were already sliding down Teagan's cheeks. "I fucking love you guys."

"Christ, Teag—language," Betty said, but her arms were wrapped around her daughters as she cried too. "I am so honored to be your mother, all of your, and this little one's grandmother, all of my grandchildren."

They stayed like that for a moment, just reveling in the female power and love in that room. This was her family, this was her identity. The Reynolds sisters were a unit that could never be broken, and here in this room, they'd never felt more bonded.

And one day, their children would all feel the same.

ACKNOWLEDGMENTS

To Nicole Resciniti, my agent—thank you for supporting me throughout every step of the writing and publishing process. I wouldn't be where I am without you, and I'm so grateful to have you by my side.

To Kay Tate, my editor—thanks for your continued help in crafting my writing and making it shine in each and every new book.

To each and every blogger and reader who keeps picking up my novels and giving them a chance—you are the real super stars. Thank you for sharing my work with your friends and continuing to make it possible for me to do my favorite thing in the world—write.

ABOUT THE AUTHOR

Photo Credit: Valerie Bey

Sarah Robinson is the Top 10 Barnes & Noble and Amazon Bestselling Author of multiple series and standalone novels, including *The Photographer Trilogy, Kavanagh Legends* series, the *Forbidden Rockers* series, and *Not a Hero: A Marine Romance*. A native of Washington, D.C., Robinson has both her bachelor's and master's degrees in forensic and clinical psychology.

9 798510 137453